HE POUNCED ON QUELCH AND DRAGGED HIM OVER ON HIS BACK

(*Page 160*)

BUNTER
THE BAD LAD

By
FRANK RICHARDS

Illustrations by
C. H. CHAPMAN

First published 1960 by Charles Skilton Ltd.

This edition published 1991 by:
HAWK BOOKS LTD
Suite 309
Canalot Studios
222 Kensal Road
London W10 5BN

ISBN 0-948248-92-0

Printed in England by Redwood Press Ltd.

CONTENTS

CONTENTS

CHAPTER 1

COKER'S LATEST

'He, he, he!'

'Hallo, hallo, hallo!'

'He, he, he!'

'What's the joke, old fat man?'

'He, he, he!'

Billy Bunter cachinnated. It was not a musical cachinnation. In fact it sounded a good deal like an alarm-clock.

Bunter, evidently, was amused. He was so amused that, instead of explaining why he cachinnated, he just went on cachinnating.

'He, he he! I say, you fellows—he, he, he!'

Harry Wharton and Co. regarded him inquiringly. The Famous Five of the Remove were seated on the bench under the old tree outside the tuck-shop at Greyfriars. They were talking cricket while they waited for the bell for class. But cricket chat was suspended, as Billy Bunter rolled up, his fat face suffused with mirth, and cachinnated unmelodiously. Clearly, something unusual was on, to throw the Owl of the Remove into such a paroxysm of merriment.

'Anything up?' asked Harry Wharton.

'He, he, he!'

'Is the upfulness terrific?' inquired Hurree Jamset Ram Singh.

'He, he, he!'

'Give it a name, fathead!' said Bob Cherry.

'I say, you fellows,' gasped Bunter. He ceased to

1

cachinnate: it was as if the alarm-clock had run down. 'I say, come on, if you want to see a lark.'

'What sort of a lark?' asked Frank Nugent.

'He, he, he!' Another explosion from Billy Bunter. 'I say, it's Coker—he, he, he.'

'Oh! Coker!' said Johnny Bull.

And the Famous Five smiled. The mere mention of Horace Coker, of the Fifth Form at Greyfriars, seemed enough to make them smile. It was true that Coker, in his own esteem, was a very serious person, to be taken very seriously indeed. But Coker was the only fellow at Greyfriars who took that view.

'What's Coker's latest?' asked Bob Cherry.

'He, he, he!' Bunter exploded again. 'I suppose old Prout's been ragging him in form—Coker's always in a row with his beak. But I say, old Prout's brought out a deck-chair—he, he, he!'

'Nothing funny in that,' said Johnny Bull.

'Unless Bunter sat in it!' remarked Bob Cherry.

'Ha, ha, ha!'

'Oh, really, Cherry! It will be funny when old Prout sits in it! I say, Quelch called to him from his study window, and Prout went in. And then Coker—he, he, he!'

'Cough it up!'

'Coker's laid an egg——!' gasped Bunter.

'What!' exclaimed all the Famous Five together.

'Coker's laid an egg in the deck-chair——'

'Coker isn't a chicken, is he?'

'I don't mean that he's laid an egg in the chair, you silly ass—I mean that he's laid an egg in the chair——'

'That's lucid, at any rate,' said Bob.

'I mean, he's laid that egg in the chair for old Prout to

sit on when he comes out! See? Fancy old Prout, when he sits down! Squash! He, he, he!'

'Ha, ha, ha!'

Billy Bunter's merriment was echoed by the Famous Five. The prospect of Mr. Prout, the plump and portly master of the Fifth, squashing an egg in his deck-chair when he sat in it, seemed to entertain them.

'Coker all over!' said Johnny Bull. 'Prout will scalp him, if he sits on that egg.'

'Let's hope he will see it before he sits down!' said Harry, laughing.

'Oh, old Prout never sees anything,' said Bunter. 'He blinks about through his specs like an owl! Awfully funny to see him blinking about through his specs like an owl, and never seeing anything.'

'Ha, ha, ha!' yelled the Famous Five. Bunter, as he made that remark, was himself blinking through his big spectacles, remarkably like an owl.

'Think it's funny to blink through specs like an owl, Bunter?' chuckled Bob.

'Yes, rather! He, he, he!'

'Well, you ought to know!' agreed Bob.

'Ha, ha, ha!'

'Oh, really, Cherry——'

'Hallo, hallo, hallo! Here comes old Coker!' ejaculated Bob Cherry, as three Fifth-form men came along the path. The juniors transferred their attention to Coker and Potter and Greene of the Fifth.

The three seniors gave no heed to the juniors under the tree. Horace Coker was walking with a disdainful nose in the air, which was often Coker's aspect. His friends seemed to be expostulating with him.

'For goodness sake, Coker——!' Potter was saying.

'You can shut up, Potter,' said Coker.

'For the love of Mike——!' urged Greene.

'You can shut up too, Greeney.'

'You will get into a row——'

'That's nothing new.'

'Prout will be wild——'

'Let him!'

'Don't do it, Coker,' urged Potter and Greene together.

'I've done it!' said Coker, calmly. 'No good jawing, you fellows. Did Prout make me sit up in form, or didn't he? Did he make out that I skewed in con, or didn't he? Did he give me that putrid Latin to write out again, or didn't he? Well, he made me sit up—now I'm going to make him sit up—on that egg! Ha, ha!'

Coker laughed.

Potter and Greene did not laugh. They were looking awfully serious. They were still expostulating with Coker, as the three walked on, and disappeared from the view of the grinning juniors.

Then Billy Bunter's fat cachinnation was heard again.

'He, he, he!' I say, you fellows, come on—old Prout will be worth watching when he sits on that egg! Squash! He, he, he!'

Bob Cherry rose from the bench.

'Look here, you chaps,' he said, 'Coker's a silly ass, and a dithering fathead, and he throws his weight about too much, and a whopping would do him good: but we don't want old Prout to scalp him. He will scalp him bald-headed if he sits on that egg!'

'No good talking sense to Coker,' said Johnny Bull.

'No: but I think I'll cut along and bag that egg, if old Prout hasn't sat on it yet,' said Bob.

To which his chums nodded assent. It was probable

that 'Coker's latest' might land him in a much larger spot of bother than Coker's rather solid brain could anticipate. Bob, who was all good-nature, was willing to take the trouble to preserve him therefrom, if he could. Only Billy Bunter raised an objection.

'I say, you fellows, don't you chip in!' exclaimed Bunter, warmly. 'No end of a lark to see Prout squashing on that egg! Let's go along and watch him. It will be funny.'

'Not for Coker,' said Harry.

'Oh, blow Coker! I tell you it will be no end funny to see the fat old donkey sit down——'

'Funny to see a fat donkey sit down?' asked Bob.

'Yes, jolly funny! He, he, he!'

'Well, here goes, then, if that's what you think funny,' said Bob: and before Billy Bunter knew what was happening, he grasped a fat neck, and hooked a fat leg. Billy Bunter sat down quite suddenly, and roared:

'Yaroooh!'

'Still think it's funny to see a fat donkey sit down?' asked Bob.

'Ha, ha, ha!'

'Ow! Beast! Wow!' spluttered the fat Owl, as he sat: apparently not finding it funny at all.

And Bob Cherry, leaving Bunter spluttering, and the other fellows laughing, cut off, to look for Prout's deck-chair and the egg that Horace Coker had laid in the seat thereof: and to save the headstrong Horace from catastrophe if there was yet time.

CHAPTER 2

EGG FOR COKER

'OH, my hat!   Too late!' murmured Bob Cherry.

He paused.

Mr. Prout's deck-chair stood in the shade by the wall, near Prout's study window.   A brown egg-shell was hardly discernible on the brown canvas.   It was as good as certain that Prout would sit on that egg before he saw it, if no friendly hand intervened.

At a little distance, Coker of the Fifth was leaning on a buttress, with an eye on that deck-chair, and an anticipatory grin on his rugged features.   His friends were no longer with him.   Probably Potter and Greene considered a safe distance judicious, when their form-master squashed that egg with his portly person.

Bob did not heed Coker.   But he had to heed Prout. Mr. Prout had come out of the House, and was coming along the path under the study windows, approaching the deck-chair with his ponderous tread, reminiscent of the 'huge earth-shaking beast' in Macaulay.

He had almost reached it.   There was no time for Bob to carry out his intention of 'bagging' that egg, unless he bagged it fairly under Prout's plump nose.

But his pause was only momentary.   Bob was quick on the uptake.   He was going to save Coker from catastrophe if he could.

He broke into a rapid run along the path, and, apparently not seeing the deck-chair in his way, crashed into it, and hurled it spinning.

6

Over went the deck-chair, folding as it went: and Coker's egg rolled harmlessly on the earth. Mr. Prout, about to sit down, gave a startled jump, as his deck-chair collapsed at his feet.

'Goodness gracious! What—what——!' gasped Mr. Prout.

'Oh! Sorry, sir!' stammered Bob.

The Fifth-form master gave him a thunderous glare.

'Cherry! You utterly clumsy and stupid boy——'

'Oh, sir!'

'Cannot you see where you are running?' thundered Mr. Prout. 'You have knocked over my chair! I have never seen anything so clumsy and stupid. Are you blind?'

'Oh! No, sir.'

'How dare you rush about the quadrangle in that disorderly manner, Cherry? I shall speak to your form-master about this, Cherry! I shall ask Mr. Quelch to deal with you. Set up that chair again at once. At once, do you hear?'

'Yes, sir! Certainly, sir.'

Bob's eye was on the egg. It had rolled within a few inches of Prout's foot, and he wondered whether Prout would notice it. His doubts on that point were soon set at rest. A brown egg-shell might escape notice on brown canvas, but it showed up quite plainly on the ground. Mr. Prout bent his head and peered at it, as Bob set up the deck-chair.

'Bless my soul! What is that?' exclaimed Mr. Prout. 'Is that an egg, Cherry?'

'It—it looks like one, sir.'

'Extraordinary!' Prout peered in astonishment at the egg. 'Yes, it is an egg—undoubtedly an egg! Who can possibly have left it lying about here? An egg—lying in

the quadrangle! Extraordinary! Bless my soul, I might
have trodden on it!'

Fortunately, it did not occur to Mr. Prout that he might
have sat on it!

'Is it yours, Cherry?'

'Oh! No! It isn't mine, sir.'

'Pick it up!' said Mr. Prout.

Bob, having set up the deck-chair, obediently picked up
the egg. Prout continued to peer at it, in surprise. It was,
in fact, rather an unusual object to be found in the Greyfriars' quad.

From his distance, Coker watched the scene, with an
expression on his face rivalling that of the fabled basilisk.
His masterly plan for making Prout 'sit up' had been washed
completely out, by a clumsy young ass of a Removite
running into the deck-chair and knocking it over! Coker
could only resolve to make that clumsy young ass sorry for
his clumsiness!

'Extraordinary!' repeated Mr. Prout, peering at the egg.
'It would have been most unpleasant to tread on such a
thing—very unpleasant indeed! Take it away, Cherry!'

'Yes, sir!'

Mr. Prout settled himself in the deck-chair, and opened
his newspaper: still puzzled by the inexplicable presence of
such an article as an egg in such a spot, and happily
unconscious of his narrow escape of sitting on it. Bob
Cherry walked away, egg in hand, very careful not to grin
till his back was turned to the master of the Fifth.

After him stalked Horace Coker.

Coker, to judge by his looks, was understudying the
Alpine climber in the poem: his brow was set, his eye
beneath flashed like a falchion from its sheath. But with
considerable self-restraint, Coker controlled his wrath, till

a safe distance from Prout had been covered. Then he pounced, clutching Bob's shoulder with a heavy hand.

'You silly, clumsy, footling young ass——!' hissed Coker.

Bob Cherry jerked his shoulder away, and jumped back. Coker looked as if assault and battery were to be the next items on the programme.

'Anything biting you, Coker?' asked Bob, cheerily.

'You clumsy little idiot!' hooted Coker. 'What do you mean by rushing into Prout's chair and knocking it over? He would have sat on that egg in another tick.'

'That's why!' explained Bob.

Coker spluttered wrath.

'Mean to say you did it on purpose?' he bawled.

'Just that, old bean,' assented Bob. 'Don't you know that your beak would have scalped you bald-headed, if he'd sat on that egg?'

'You cheeky little tick——'

'You'd have been up for six, fathead! Now thank me nicely for keeping you out of a row!' suggested Bob.

Horace Coker looked anything but thankful or nice. So far from thanking Bob for services rendered, he gave him a glare that was absolutely ferocious.

'So you butted in on purpose, you cheeky fag?' he roared. 'By gum, I'll jolly well show you whether you can butt in. I'm going to smack your head for your cheek, see?'

Coker made a stride, with a large hand extended. Bob Cherry made a nimble backward jump, and the large hand swept the empty air. Coker made another stride, and Bob another backward jump.

Then Coker rushed.

In another moment, Bob Cherry would have been in his mighty grasp. Bob was a very sturdy fellow for the Lower

Fourth: but he was a junior, and Coker a Fifth-form
senior: and an out-size even for the Fifth. Coker's mighty
grasp would have crumpled him up, had it reached him.

But it did not reach him.

At the psychological moment, Bob hurled the egg.

It was Coker's egg, and perhaps he wanted it back.
But assuredly he did not want it back in the way he received
it. Bob's action was swift, and his aim was accurate.

Crack! Squash!

That egg had been intended to crack and squash under
the portly person of Mr. Prout. Instead of which, it
cracked and squashed on Horace Coker's rather prominent
nose. Its contents spread over his features. Coker's
rugged face was suddenly clothed in egg.

'Ooooooh!' spluttered Coker.

He tottered, clawing wildly at the egg.

'Ha, ha, ha!' roared Bob.

'Urrrggh! I'm all eggy! Ooooooh! Why, I'll smash
you—I'll spiflicate you—I—I'll—groogh——'

Bob Cherry did not wait to be smashed or spiflicated.
He cut off without delay to rejoin his friends. He was
likely to need their aid if Coker pursued.

But Coker did not pursue. He clawed at egg. Even
Coker's solid brain realized that what he needed just then
was not so much vengeance on a cheeky Remove junior, as
a wash! His face was all eggy: and yolk was running
down into his collar. Breathing wrath—and egg—and
dabbing at an eggy face with an eggy handkerchief, Coker
tramped away to the House for the wash he really needed.

CHAPTER 3

BAFFLED BUNTER

'Bunter!'

'Oh!' gasped Billy Bunter.

Bunter was startled.

He had not, at that moment, expected to meet his form-master, Mr. Quelch. He met him quite unexpectedly.

The bell was ringing for class. Greyfriars fellows, in all quarters, were heading for their form-rooms. The Remove had already gathered at their form-door: with one exception. That exception was the fattest member of the form. Billy Bunter, instead of gathering with the rest, had heaved his considerable weight up the staircase, and was about to cross the landing in the direction of the Fifth-form studies, when that sharp rap fell on his fat ears.

He blinked round at Mr. Quelch through his big spectacles. Quelch was coming across the landing, no doubt on his way down to deal with his form. He was naturally surprised, and not pleased, to see a member of the Remove heading away from the form-room, instead of towards it, when the bell was ringing. Mr. Quelch was a firm believer in that punctuality which is said to be the politeness of princes. Bunter, evidently, was disregarding punctuality. He was going to be late for class—had not Quelch met him on the landing.

But for that unexpected meeting, it was, from Billy Bunter's point of view, worth while. Billy Bunter was aware that Gosling, the ancient Greyfriars' porter, had taken a parcel up to Coker's study in the Fifth. And Billy

Bunter, who was constitutionally incapable of resisting tuck—anybody's tuck—had designs on that parcel.

It had seemed to Bunter a most propitious moment. With the bell ringing, announcing the end of 'break', and everybody heading for class, the studies of course were deserted. There was—or should have been—nobody about in the studies. There might be lines from Quelch, if a fellow was late: but it was worth lines, if they accrued, to have first 'go' at that parcel. It looked like plain sailing, to Bunter—till that sharp voice rapped on the landing. Then, as a poet has already expressed it, a change came o'er the spirit of his dream.

'Where are you going, Bunter?' rapped Mr. Quelch.

'Oh! Nowhere, sir——!' stammered Bunter.

'What?'

'I—I—I mean, I—I wasn't going to Coker's study——'

'Coker's study!'

'Oh! No, sir! I—I—I—I mean——'

A pair of gimlet-eyes glinted at the fat Owl.

'You were going to a Fifth-form study, Bunter? Why?'

'Oh! No, sir! Yes, sir! I—I mean, Coker asked me to fetch a book for him, sir.'

'You should not have done so, Bunter, when the bell is ringing for class. Did you not hear the bell?'

'No, sir! I—I mean, yes, sir.'

'Go to your form-room immediately, Bunter.'

'Yes, sir!' groaned Bunter.

The fat Owl revolved on his axis. He descended the stairs dismally, Mr. Quelch following him down. The bell was giving its last clang, as they arrived at the door of the Remove form-room, where the rest of the Remove were gathered. Mr. Quelch let in his form: and Bunter rolled in with the rest, not late for class, after all!

The lesson, in third school that day, was History. Harry Wharton and Co., and other fellows, came in cheerfully enough, prepared to tolerate the annals of their native land till the welcome moment of dismissal came. But the fattest face in the form was not cheerful.

Billy Bunter was seldom keen on dead-and-gone kings and queens, and battles long ago. His interest now was down to absolute zero. Whether Cromwell had cut off King Charles' head, or whether King Charles had cut off Cromwell's, Bunter couldn't have cared less. Something much more modern was in Bunter's fat mind. Actually, he had heard Coker mention to Potter and Greene that he had unpacked bananas from that parcel. Bunter liked bananas. As likely as not, in fact more likely than not, Coker and Co. would wolf those bananas after third school. In such circumstances, William George Bunter could hardly concentrate his fat intellect on lessons. Never had Quelch's valuable instruction seemed to him more weary, stale, flat, and unprofitable.

'If you please, sir—!' It was a sudden squeak from Bunter.

A gimlet-eye fixed on him.

'Well?'

'If you please, sir, I—I forgot my book, sir——'

'You should not have forgotten your book, Bunter.'

'Oh! Yes, sir! No, sir! Mumum-may I go up to my study, sir, and fetch it.'

'You may not, Bunter. You may look at Todd's book. And if you have forgotten to bring your book to the formroom, Bunter, you will take fifty lines.'

'Oh!' gasped Bunter. 'I—I—I mean——'

'That will do, Bunter.'

'I—I—I mean, I—I've just found it, sir—I—I—I hadn't forgotten it after all, sir!' gasped Bunter.

Mr. Quelch gave the fat Owl an expressive look. Some of the Remove fellows glanced round at him. Skinner winked at Snoop. Bob Cherry grinned. It was fairly plain, to many fellows, that what Billy Bunter really wanted was an excuse for getting out of class. A forgotten book was the first excuse that had come into his fat mind. It had failed to work the oracle, so to speak, and it would have been wise of Bunter to leave it at that.

But Billy Bunter belonged to the class of persons who rush in where angels fear to tread. Wisdom was not Bunter's long suit. Instead of taking warning from Quelch's expressive look, and giving some attention to the lesson, Bunter devoted all his fat intellectual powers to thinking up another dodge for getting at the bananas in Coker's study.

'Please, sir——!' Bunter re-started after an interval.

'Did you speak, Bunter?' asked Mr. Quelch, ominously.

'Yes, sir! If you please, sir, I remember I forgot to turn off the tap in the Remove passage, sir—may I go up and turn it off, sir.'

'You have left a tap running!' exclaimed Mr. Quelch.

'Yes, sir! I'm so sorry, sir! Mum-mum-may I—I go up and turn it off, sir? It—it might flood over the sink, sir.'

'Wharton!'

'Yes, sir.'

'Please go up to the Remove passage, and turn off the tap that Bunter has left running.'

'Yes, sir,' said Harry. He rose in his place.

'Bunter! You will take a hundred lines for having left a tap running.'

'Oh, crikey! I—I—I—I mean, sir, I—I remember now,

I—I didn't leave it running, sir!' stammered Bunter.
'I—I've just remembered that I turned it off, sir.'

'Oh, my hat!' murmured Bob Cherry.

'Upon my word!' said Mr. Quelch. 'You may remain
in your place, Wharton. Bunter, you will bring your lines
to my study after tea.'

'Oh, really, sir! I——'

'That will do, Bunter! It appears to me,' said Mr.
Quelch, grimly, 'that you are thinking of other matters,
Bunter, instead of paying attention to the lesson.'

'Oh, no, sir! Not at all, sir!' groaned Bunter. 'I heard
every word you were saying, sir! Every word, sir.'

'I am glad of that,' said Mr. Quelch, still more grimly,
'as I shall now ask you some questions on the subject,
Bunter.'

'What was it, Bunter, that Oliver Cromwell said when the
mace was placed on the table in the House of Commons?'

Billy Bunter blinked at him. As Quelch had just been
dealing with that very episode, the fat Owl should really
have been able to answer that question without hesitation.
But with his fat mind concentrated on bananas, Quelch's
voice had been, to Bunter, nothing but a drone in his fat
ears, which he passed by like the idle wind which he regarded
not. Now he wished that he had regarded it a little.

'Oh! He—he—he said——!' stammered Bunter.
Pause!

'Well?' rapped Mr. Quelch.

Billy Bunter cudgelled his fat brains. He was aware
that the great Oliver had walked into the House of Commons, recklessly interrupting the flow of Parliamentary
eloquence in that building. Apparently he had said something when the mace was placed on the table: probably
some historic remark, as Quelch made a point of it. Various

historic remarks were mixed up vaguely in Billy Bunter's uncertain memory, but he was very vague about which was which. But he had to make a shot at it.

'He—he said, "Kiss me, Hardy"!' ventured Bunter.

'Ha, ha, ha!' came a howl from the Remove. Really, they could not help it, even under Quelch's gimlet-eye. That answer was unusually rich, even for Bunter.

'Silence in the class!' rapped Mr. Quelch. 'Bunter! How dare you make such an answer?'

'I—I—I mean——I—I don't mean that he said "Kiss me, Hardy!" sir!' gasped Bunter, realizing that his shot had missed the mark. 'I—I mean——'

'What do you mean?'

'I—I mean, he—he said, "Up, Guards, and at 'em!"' gasped Bunter.

'Bless my soul! You have evidently not been listening to a word during this lesson, Bunter. I will not allow such inattention in form, Bunter. You are answering me at random, Bunter,' thundered Mr. Quelch.

'Oh, lor'! Oh, no, sir! I—I didn't mean that he said "Up, Guards, and at 'em!"' stuttered Bunter. 'I—I meant to say——'

'Unless you give me the correct answer immediately, Bunter——'

'Oh, yes, sir!' groaned Bunter. 'I—I know what he said, sir, when they put the tace on the mable—I mean when they put the mace on the table. He—he—he said——'

'Well?' Quelch shot out that monosyllable like a bullet.

'He—he said, "If I had but served King Alfred as I have served Pontius Pilate," sir——'

'Ha, ha, ha!'

'Silence!' hooted Mr. Quelch. 'This boy's absurdities are not a subject for merriment.'

'Aren't they just!' murmured Bob Cherry, and his comrades grinned.

'Cherry!'

'Oh! Yes, sir!' stammered Bob. His murmured remark had certainly not been intended for Quelch's ears. But those ears seemed unusually sharp that morning.

'Did you speak, Cherry?'

'Oh! Yes, sir.'

'And what did you say, Cherry?'

'I—I—I said, "Aren't they just!" sir!' stammered Bob.

'Indeed!' said Mr. Quelch. 'Then you will write out that remark a hundred times after class, Cherry.'

'Oh! Yes, sir!' mumbled Bob.

No more murmured remarks were likely to be made in the Remove during that lesson. The gimlet-eyes turned back on the hapless Owl. But during the moment or two that Quelch had been giving his attention to Bob, Peter Todd, greatly daring, had ventured to whisper in a fat ear.

'Take away that bauble,' whispered Peter.

It was a brief, hurried whisper, and perhaps the fat ear did not quite catch it. The gimlet-eye was on the fat Owl again.

'Now, Bunter——' rumbled Mr. Quelch.

'Yes, sir, I know what he said, sir,' said Bunter, quite brightly. 'He said, "Take away that bubble," sir.'

'That what?' ejaculated Mr. Quelch.

'That bubble, sir——'

'That bubble!' repeated Mr. Quelch, almost dazedly.

'Yes, sir—take away that bubble——'

'Upon my word! Bunter, in addition to the lines I have given you, you will write out, fifty times, the sentence, "Take away that bauble." And now, Bunter, if you do not give attention, I shall cane you.'

That was enough even for William George Bunter. He could not quite dismiss Coker's bananas from mind: but he gave attention to the lesson, instead of thinking up new dodges for getting out of form. He had to leave those bananas till after class: at the risk of Coker and Co. 'wolfing' them. And when, after third school, he blinked into Coker's study in the Fifth, and unexpectedly beheld Horace Coker there, sitting at the table with a pen in his hand, and a thoughtful frown on his rugged brow, Bunter's feelings were really too deep for words. The only consolation was that the bananas were still on the table, unheeded by Coker, which indicated that there might be a chance for an unscrupulous fat Owl later: for the present, it was a baffled Bunter!

After dinner, however, a prowling fat Owl found Coker's study untenanted: and the bananas still there! They did not remain there!

But——!

CHAPTER 4

NO BANANAS FOR BUNTER

'Stand——'

'Eh!'

'And deliver——'

'Ha, ha, ha!'

Billy Bunter stood—he had to stand, as Bob Cherry's sturdy figure barred his way across the Remove landing. But he did not deliver.

Harry Wharton and Co. were coming across the landing from the Remove studies, when Bunter happened to appear. The fat Owl of the Remove emerged upon the landing from the Fifth-form passage, rolling across towards the Remove quarters.   Under either fat arm, he carried a large bunch of bananas.   Hence Bob's playful injunction to "stand and deliver!"'

'Whose bananas?' asked Harry Wharton, laughing.

'Mine!' hooted Bunter.

'Where did you get them?'

'Oh, really, Wharton!   You jolly well know that I have jolly big parcels from Bunter Court——'

'I don't!'

'Beast!   Look here, let a fellow pass——'

'Stand and deliver!' grinned Bob.

'Gerrout of the way!' exclaimed Bunter, with a hurried blink through his big spectacles towards the staircase. 'Coker might come up any minute——'

'What about it?' chuckled Bob.

'Oh!   Nothing!   Still, if he saw these bananas, he might

19

think they were his. You know him—suspicious beast!
Will you let a fellow pass?' howled Bunter.

The fat Owl dodged to Bob's right, in the hope of circum-
navigating him. Harry Wharton blocked the way. Then
he dodged to Bob's left. Johnny Bull blocked the way.
Then he backed away—and backed into Frank Nugent and
Hurree Jamset Ram Singh. Five grinning faces surrounded
him. There was no escape for a fat Owl.

'I say, you fellows, no larks!' gasped Bunter. 'I say,
I—I was going to ask you to whack out these bananas with
me. Come along to my study, and I'll whack out the lot,
honest Injun.'

'You fat brigand,' said Harry Wharton. 'Have you
been snooping in Coker's study?'

'Of—of course not! I never knew Coker had had a
parcel from his Aunt Judy. How could I? I never heard
him mention it to Potter and Greene, if that's what you
think. These bananas came in a parcel this morning from
my uncle Carter at Folkestone——'

'As well as from Bunter Court?' asked Bob Cherry.

'I—I—I mean Bunter Court——'

'You never had a parcel this morning,' said Johnny Bull.

'I—I mean yesterday——'

'Now, let's have it clear,' said Bob. 'Those bananas
came from Bunter Court this morning, and they came from
Folkestone yesterday. Is that it?'

'Yes—I—I mean——'

'Ha, ha, ha!'

'Walk him back to Coker's study with them,' said
Johnny Bull.

'I—I say, you fellows, they ain't Coker's. I haven't
been near his study, and he hadn't left them on the table
there, and I certainly never saw them when I looked in.

Besides, I never looked in. I was down in Quelch's study when I was there—I mean when I wasn't there——'

'Take his other ear, Bob,' said Harry.

'Yow-ow-ow!' roared Bunter, as a fat ear was annexed by a finger and thumb: another finger and thumb immediately following suit on the other fat ear. 'Wow! Leggo my ears!'

'Come on,' said Harry.

'Shan't!' howled Bunter.

'Well, your ears are jolly well coming,' said Bob. 'You can suit yourself about coming along with them.'

'Ha, ha, ha!'

'Yow-ow-ow!' wailed Bunter.

He rolled back towards the Fifth-form studies, between Bob Cherry and the captain of the Remove. His fat ears, in a firm grip, travelled in that direction: and Bunter apparently decided to go with them! He emitted a series of indignant squeaks as he went.

Bob Cherry and Harry Wharton walked him up the passage to Coker's study, Johnny Bull and Nugent and the nabob of Bhanipur walking behind grinning. Billy Bunter was not in the least particular whose tuck he packed inside the most extensive circumference in the Remove: all was grist that came to his mill. The fat Owl really seemed quite unable to realize that there were rights of property in tuck. But the Famous Five were a little more particular on such points: and those bananas were going back where they belonged. The grip on Billy Bunter's fat ears did not relax, till he was walked into Horace Coker's study.

'Here you are,' said Bob. 'Now disgorge, you fat octopus.'

'Leggo my ears!'

'Not till you leggo the bananas.'

'Ha, ha, ha!'

'I—I—I say, you fellows, I'll go halves——'

'Let go those bananas, you fat chump, or I shall lug at that flap you call an ear—like that!'

'Yarooooh!'

One 'lug' at the fat ear was enough for Billy Bunter. He landed those bunches of bananas on the study table. It was a painful parting: but not quite so painful as lugs at his fat ears.

'Hallo, hallo, hallo, what's that?' exclaimed Bob Cherry, his eyes falling on a sheet of impot paper on the table, as the bananas landed.

'Oh, my hat!' exclaimed Harry Wharton.

'That ass Coker——!'

'If Prout saw that——!'

'The rowfulness would be terrific.'

The juniors stared at the paper. On it was written a single line, in the well-known scrawling 'fist' of Horace Coker. Coker's hand-writing was easily recognizable, from its resemblance to the trail of a fly that had crawled out of an inkpot. That line ran:

There was an old duffer named Prout.

It looked like the first line of a 'limerick'. Coker of the Fifth, it seemed, was trying his hand at verse. But apparently inspiration had failed him after one line, for that was all there was of it. But that one line, if Mr. Prout had happened to visit Coker's study, was enough to land Coker in bad trouble. Coker, no doubt, regarded his form-master as an 'old duffer': but Mr. Prout's wrath, if he saw himself so described, was likely to resemble that of Achilles, to Greece the direful spring of woes unnumbered. Harry Wharton and Co. gazed at it almost in horror.

'The howling ass!' exclaimed Bob. 'Prout would walk him off to the Head if he saw that.'

'The dithering dunderhead!' said Harry. 'Just like Coker to leave it there for anybody to see.'

'The terrific fathead!' said Hurree Jamset Ram Singh.

'Coker's the man to ask for it!' said Bob. 'He isn't satisfied with setting eggs for Prout to hatch. Whoppings aren't good enough for him: he wants to go up to the Head to be bunked. Well, I did him one good turn this morning —now I'll do him another.'

Bob Cherry picked up the inkpot, and up-ended it over that sheet of impot paper. Coker's efforts at versification disappeared from existence under a sea of ink.

'That's that,' said Bob.

'Ha, ha, ha!'

'Now come on—Coker might be cross, if he found us in his study with his inkpot upset. Come on, Bunter.'

Unwillingly, Billy Bunter came on. The Famous Five walked him back to the landing. At the head of the stairs, he stopped.

'You fellows going out?' he asked.

'Yes: come on.'

'I've got to go to my study. I've got to get a book for class.'

'Okay—we'll come with you.'

'I—I mean, I've go to do some lines for Quelch. You fellows don't want to stick around while I'm doing my lines. You just cut on——'

'Ha, ha, ha!'

'Blessed if I see anything to cackle at. Look here, I've got to get that book—I mean I've got to do those lines——'

'And you wouldn't go back to Coker's study for those bananas?'

'Oh! No! I—I've got to get my lines for class—I mean, I've got to do a book for Quelch—I—I mean——'

'We know exactly what you mean, old fat man,' chuckled Bob. 'You're going for a walk with us till the bell goes for class. Come on.'

Billy Bunter blinked, with an infuriated blink, at five grinning faces. But there was no help for it. In the midst of the Famous Five, the fat Owl descended the stairs, and rolled out into the quadrangle. Billy Bunter's company was not, as a rule, much sought after by the chums of the Remove: in fact, as a rule, the less they had of it the more they enjoyed it. But on the present occasion, Bunter's company, till class, was essential, if Coker's bananas were to remain Coker's property. So they walked Billy Bunter out into the quad, heedless of the almost deadly blinks he gave them through his big spectacles, and there were no bananas for Bunter.

CHAPTER 5

POETIC!

'Oh, scissors!' gasped Horace Coker.

Coker's rugged face registered alarm.

Potter and Greene looked at him. They could see no cause for alarm. They had a back view of Prout. But there was nothing alarming, to them, in Mr. Prout seen from the south, as it were.

But Coker looked horrified.

The three Fifth-form men were coming up to their study. Coker wanted to get on with that unfinished limerick. Potter and Greene, wholly and utterly uninterested in Coker's limerick, were interested in bananas. There was plenty of time before class for Coker to concentrate on verse, and for his friends to concentrate on bananas. So there they were, coming into the Fifth-form passage from the landing, about ten minutes after Billy Bunter's enforced departure with the Famous Five. Ahead of them, in that passage, was a portly figure, of which they had only a back view, as it turned in at the doorway of Coker's study.

Why Prout had come up to that study, Potter and Greene did not know. Neither did they care. But Horace Coker, evidently, cared.

'Oh, scissors!' he repeated. 'That's Prout!'

'What about it?' asked Potter.

'He's gone into our study.'

'Why shouldn't he?' asked Greene.

'If he sees what's on the table!' gasped Coker.

'Rot!' said Potter. 'I expect he's come up about your

25

impot. You haven't handed it in. He told you to write the lesson over again. That's what he's after. You don't fancy he'd scoff the bananas, do you?'

'Oh, don't be an ass!' hissed Coker. 'I'm not thinking about bananas. I'm thinking about my limerick. I left it on the table. I'd written only one line, so far—I had to chuck it when the bell went for dinner——'

'What was the line?'

'There was an old duffer named Prout!'

'Oh, holy smoke! You've written that and left it on the study table!' exclaimed Potter. 'And Prout's in the study—Oh, crumbs.'

'Look out for squalls!' said Greene.

'He mayn't have seen it yet,' said Coker, hopefully. 'Come on—he's as blind as a bat, and he mayn't have spotted it. Might shove a book or something over it before he sees it. Hurry up.'

Coker hurried up the passage. Potter and Greene hurried after him. If Prout's eyes had fallen on that description of himself, there was no doubt at all that the thunder would roll. Possibly there was a chance yet of averting the calamity.

As they entered the study, they again had a back view of Prout. He was at the study table, scanning it, apparently looking for something. Potter and Greene exchanged a hopeless look. Coker caught his breath. Prout was short-sighted: but he was scanning the table, and it was simply impossible that he could miss what lay there.

He turned from the table. His frowning glance fixed on Coker.

'Coker!' rumbled Prout.

'Yes, sir!' said Coker, faintly. He waited for the thunder to roll.

'Coker! It appears that you have not yet written your imposition. I see no sign of it here.'

'Oh! No! N-n-no, sir,' gasped Coker. He wondered dizzily why Prout was talking about his impot, when he must have seen that limerick line.

'You were directed to bring it to my study before class, Coker.'

'Oh! Yes, sir!'

'You have not done so.'

'Oh! No, sir.'

'Neither do I see it here,' said Mr. Prout, sternly. 'You have not even commenced to write it, Coker.'

'I—I—I——'

'This will not do, Coker! I warn you, Coker, that this will not do.' Mr. Prout had a way of repeating his remarks. No doubt he had an impression that they were worth hearing twice. 'You are a careless, thoughtless, impertinent boy, Coker. Careless, thoughtless, and impertinent, Coker. I warn you very seriously that this will not do. I will be obeyed by the boys of my form. Your imposition is doubled, Coker. You will write it out twice, and bring it to me this evening. Take warning, Coker!'

Coker could only blink at him. It looked as if Prout hadn't seen that limerick line after all. How he could have missed it, was a mystery. But it looked as if he had.

'That is all now, Coker!' added Prout. 'But I warn you, Coker, to take care. I warn you very seriously, Coker, to take care.'

With that, Prout rolled out of the study, frowning: leaving the three Fifth-formers staring at one another as his ponderous footsteps died away down the passage.

Then Coker made a jump for the table. And then he understood, as he saw a sea of ink blotting the paper on

C

which the limerick line had been written. Not a syllable of that line was visible through the ink.

'Oh!' gasped Coker. 'He never saw it! Thank goodness one of you clumsy fatheads upset the ink over it.'

'I didn't upset the ink,' said Potter.

'And I didn't, either,' said Greene.

'Oh, don't talk rot,' said Coker, testily. 'It's jolly lucky you did—but you can see that you did, I suppose, as the ink's smothered all over my limerick. I wish you fellows wouldn't keep on arguing.'

'I tell you I never upset the ink——'

'And I tell you that I never did, either——'

'Oh, perhaps it upset itself!' said Coker, sarcastically. 'Perhaps that inkpot's a sort of Sputnik, and can buzz about on its own. Think that's likely?'

'I tell you——'

'And I tell you——'

'Pack it up,' said Coker. 'I'm glad you upset the ink, as Prout came nosing in and might have seen my limerick, and that's enough. Don't jaw any more. I'm going to finish that limerick now. You fellows can help yourselves to the bananas, if you like.'

That, at least, Potter and Greene were quite prepared to do, and they lost no time about it. They started on the bananas. Coker, apparently feeling the poetic urge within, was above bananas. He sat down at the table, selected a fresh sheet of paper, and dipped a pen in the ink. His rugged brow was corrugated with thought. Mental effort did not, as a matter of fact, come easily to Horace Coker. His powerful intellect moved to slow motion—very slow indeed.

'You're not going to write that rot over again, surely, Coker,' said Potter. 'If Prout had seen it——'

'Prout didn't see it,' said Coker. 'But he's going to.'

'What?' exclaimed Potter and Greene together.

'Prout's going to see it, and it's jolly well going to make him sit up, when I've finished it,' said Coker, coolly. 'But he's not going to see it in my fist, see? He can guess at who did it—and go on guessing as long as he likes. If he saw it in my fist, I shouldn't wonder if he walked me off to the head——'

'He jolly well would.'

'Well, he won't have the chance. After I've finished making it up, I'm going to copy it out on a typewriter. There's a typewriter in Quelch's study, and a fellow could nip in and use it, while Quelch is gone out on one of his grinds. I'm no fool!' added Coker—a statement which it was simply impossible for his friends to credit.

'For goodness sake, Coker, chuck it up!' urged Greene.

'I'll watch it!' said Coker. 'The fact is, that it's time somebody told that old ass what an ass he is. Didn't he rag me in form this morning, making out that I skewed? Hasn't he just doubled my impot? I'll show him! Now shut up while I do this limerick.'

'But look here——'

'Don't argue! Just shut up.'

Argument, clearly, was wasted on Horace James Coker. Potter and Greene shut up, and concentrated on the bananas. Coker wrinkled a rugged brow over his task. Having written once more 'There was an old duffer named Prout', he seemed rather at a loss. Inspiration did not seem to come.

'Got a rhyme for Prout, you chaps?' he asked, at last.

'Lots of rhymes for Prout,' said Greene. 'There's clout——'

'Clout's no use.'

'Or lout——'

Coker shook his head, frowning.

'Can't call a man a lout,' he said. 'There's a limit. After all, he's our beak. Lout wouldn't do! I'm surprised at you suggesting calling Prout a lout, Greeney. Rotten bad form.'

'I didn't!' yelled Greene. 'You asked for a rhyme, that's all.'

'Don't yell at me, Billy Greene. I've told you it's rotten bad form to suggest calling Prout a lout——'

'I never——!' shrieked Greene.

'Don't say any more, Greene—I've told you it's rotten bad form, and that's enough. Lout, indeed! Fat lot of use you chaps are, when a chap's bottled for a rhyme, and all you can do is to suggest calling our beak a lout! If you can't help, keep quiet!'

Coker bent his head over his task again. The look that William Greene fixed on that bent head, indicated that Greene was powerfully tempted to jam it down on the table —hard! However, he refrained from that drastic action, and continued operations on the bananas.

'Enormously podgy and stout!' exclaimed Coker, suddenly. Inspiration had accrued, at last! With a cheery grin, Coker wrote down that inspired line.

'Not too bad, so far, you chaps,' he said. 'Listen! There was an old duffer named Prout, enormously podgy and stout. Ha, Ha! Now something about his jawing so much—what do you fellows think?'

'I think we'll go for a trot before class,' said Potter.

'Same here,' assented Greene.

Coker had not finished the limerick. But Potter and Greene had finished the bananas. So, as their interest in that limerick was absolutely nil, there remained no reason for lingering in the study. They moved to the door.

'Hold on,' said Coker, 'I'm bottled over the next line. You're not much use, as you haven't much sense, but you might help. Look here——'

'Well, I can give you one tip!' said Greene, with a wink at Potter.

'What's that?'

'Don't forget to leave it on the table, for Prout to see if he comes up again!' said Greene.

With that, Potter and Greene departed, grinning. Coker, frowning, was left to finish his limerick on his own.

CHAPTER 6

COKER'S LIMERICK

'POMPOUS old ass!' said Coker.

'Better not tell him so,' murmured Potter.

'I've a jolly good mind to.'

Potter winked at Greene, with the eye furthest from Coker. Greene grinned. If Horace Coker had a jolly good mind to tell Mr. Prout that he was a pompous old ass, it was probable that he had a jollier good mind not to do so.

Coker had joined his friends in the quad. There was a satisfied expression on Coker's face. His mental wrestlings in the study had produced results. That limerick was finished. It was finished to Coker's satisfaction. It was going to make Prout sit up. It was going to make him wild. In fact, it was going to make him rage. Which, in Horace Coker's opinion, was a consummation devoutly to be wished.

Mr. Prout, passing at a little distance, did not hear Coker's remark. Coker's eye gleamed after him, as he rolled on. Often and often was Coker in a spot of bother with his form-master. Prout, a really kindly gentleman at heart, could be patient with obtuseness. But obstinacy added to obtuseness was too much for Prout's patience. Coker had been 'through it' that morning in form with Prout. Since then he had had his imposition doubled. Coker was going to 'get his own back' on Prout: and Coker knew how.

'The fact is, I'm telling him so, in that limerick,' went on Coker. 'I've put it in the first line. Listen to this, you chaps.'

Coker drew a crumpled sheet of paper from his pocket. On it, in Coker's sprawling fist, was written that completed limerick. He proceeded to read it out to his friends—casting a glance round first to make quite sure that Prout was out of hearing. Even Coker realized that he had better not let Prout hear it.

There's a pompous old duffer named Prout,
Enormously podgy and stout,
    He talks awful rot,
    And he never knows what
He is talking and talking about.

'What price that?' grinned Coker. 'Ha, ha!'

Evidently, Coker was pleased with his limerick. But if he expected Potter and Greene to join in his merriment, he was disappointed. They looked horrified.

'You ass!' gasped Potter.

'You fathead!' breathed Greene.

'Doesn't it hit Prout off to a T?' demanded Coker. 'Isn't it Prout all over? Ain't he a pompous old duffer? Ain't he podgy and stout? Don't he talk awful rot? And does he ever know what he's talking about? Ha, ha!'

'If Prout saw that——!' breathed Potter.

'He's going to see it!' said Coker, calmly. 'I'm going to stick it on his study table for him to see.'

'You mad ass!' howled Greene. 'Don't you know that Prout would walk you off straight to the Head, and that you'd be bunked for it?'

'Bunked so fast it would make your head swim!' said Potter.

'I think I told you I'm no fool!' answered Coker. 'This isn't the copy I'm going to leave for Prout. He would know my fist at once. I've told you what I'm going to do—

I'm going to type it out on Quelch's typewriter for Prout.
He won't know who did it.   He can think it was Quelch, if
he likes—ha, ha!'

'Better put a match to it,' said Potter.

'I'll watch it.'

'Prout will be as mad as a hatter if he sees that——'

'That's what I want.'

'For goodness sake, Coker.'   Potter almost pleaded.
'This is worse than putting an egg for him to sit on.   Chuck
it, for goodness sake.'

'Likely, after all the trouble I've taken,' said Coker,
disdainfully.   'I'll show him!   You heard him in the form-
room this morning, making out that I skewed in con.
Making out that "per noctem plurima volvens" doesn't
mean turning over in bed——'

'But it doesn't!' howled Greene.

'Don't be an ass, Greeney, if you can help it.'

'It means turning things over in the mind during the
night.   Prout told you so.' hooted Potter.

'I know he did.'

'Well, think you know better than Prout?'

'I hope so.'

'Oh, my hat!' said Potter.   Clearly, it was not of much
use to argue with Horace Coker.   A fellow who knew better
than his form-master was beyond argument.

'Prout don't know all the Latin he makes out,' went on
Coker.   'Schoolmasters don't know a lot, if you come to
that.   Virgil is pretty poor stuff, I know: but even Virgil
meant something when he wrote his tosh, and when he wrote
"per noctem plurima volvens" he meant turning over in
bed, and if Prout don't know it, he ought to be glad that
there's a fellow in his form who can tell him.   Now I've

got to write the tosh out twice over, because Prout doesn't
know what he's talking about.   I'll show him.'

'Coker, old man——!'

'Coker, old chap——'

'No good jawing,' said Coker, decisively.   'I know
what I'm going to do.   Quelch always goes out for a grind
after class.   As soon as he's gone out, I shall nip into his
study, and type this out on his machine.   There won't be a
clue.   When Prout finds it in his study, he can guess and
guess and guess at who did it, and go on guessing.   Fancy
his face!   Ha, ha!'

'For goodness sake, Coker——'

'And that ain't all!' went on Coker.   'I'll type a couple
of copies while I'm about it, and leave one on the table in
Common-room for all the beaks to see!   I've got it in for
Prout, I can tell you.   He never sat on that egg this morning,
owing to that cheeky young scoundrel Cherry butting in.
But will this make him wild?   Fancy Quelch, and Hacker,
and Twigg, and Wiggins, reading it in Common-room, and
sniggering over it—why, old Pompous will be foaming at
the mouth—ha, ha.'

Coker chuckled, loud and long.   The prospect of the
stately and portly Prout foaming at the mouth seemed to
entertain him immensely.

'Listen, you chaps—I'll read it out to you again!' he
added.

'That's all right—we've heard it——' said Potter.

'I said listen!' snapped Coker.

And he proceeded to read out that brilliant limerick a
second time.

> 'There's a pompous old duffer named Prout,
> Enormously podgy and——

At that point came an interruption. It was a loud yell from a little distance. Some of the old Greyfriars' elms hid what was going on: but that yell came loud and clear:

'Yaroooh!'

Coker frowned darkly.

'Those Remove fags!' he said. 'Cheeky little beasts— they think nothing of kicking up a shindy in the quad. I'll jolly soon stop them.'

It was one of Horace Coker's many gifts that he never could mind his own business. Something was going on behind the elms—apparently a shindy of some sort; that frantic yell sounded like it. A Sixth-form prefect would doubtless have given it a look-in; but it had nothing whatever to do with a Fifth-form fellow. That made no difference to Coker. He was going to stop it! Throwing his weight about was one of Coker's ways which did not make him popular with the juniors.

'Come on, you two!' added Coker.

'Oh, give them a miss,' said Potter.

'I said come on!' snapped Coker.

And he strode away, with a frowning brow, to see what was going on, and put a stop to it. No doubt he expected Potter and Greene to follow. But they did not follow.

'Feel like getting mixed up in a row with a mob of fags, Greeney?' asked Potter.

'Not a lot,' said Greene.

'Same here! If Coker wants a shindy with Remove fags, he can have it all to himself, what?'

'Exactly!' agreed Greene.

And they walked away in another direction.

CHAPTER 7

BEASTLY FOR BUNTER

'BEASTS!' roared Billy Bunter.

'Ha, ha, ha!'

'Will you let a fellow pass?'

'Not so's you'd notice it.'

'I've got to see Quelch! I've got to go to his study before class——'

'You won't see him in his study: he's trotting in the quad.'

'I—I mean, I've got to see the Head——'

'Ha, ha, ha!'

'I can't keep the Head waiting——'

'Ha, ha, ha!'

Billy Bunter glared round at a circle of grinning faces, with a glare that might almost have endangered his spectacles. The fat Owl was the centre of that circle: hemmed in, as it were. Not only the Famous Five surrounded him—several other Remove fellows had joined the circle—Vernon-Smith, Peter Todd, Squiff, Tom Brown, and Lord Mauleverer. All of them seemed very much amused —in contrast to Bunter, who was not amused at all.

It was almost time for the bell to ring for class. Minutes were precious now, from Billy Bunter's point of view. Coker and Co. might go up to their study and scoff those bananas before class. That, in point of fact, had already happened: but the fat Owl, unaware of it, still yearned for those bananas: and his little round eyes gleamed wrath through his big round spectacles, at the grinning juniors surrounding him.

'If you jolly well don't let me pass, Bob Cherry——'

'No "if" about that!' grinned Bob. 'You're jolly well stopping here till the bell goes.'

'I—I—I'm not going to Coker's study——'

'You're not!' agreed Harry Wharton.

'The notfulness is terrific,' chuckled Hurree Jamset Ram Singh.

'Besides, look what a beast Coker is. It would serve him right to bag his bananas,' urged Bunter. 'Look how he throws his weight about. He smacked my head the other day.'

'Nothing in it to damage,' said Bob.

'Beast! If you jolly well don't let me pass, I'll jolly well punch your nose, Bob Cherry.'

'Somebody give Bunter a bunk up!' said Bob.

'Ha, ha, ha!'

'I tell you I've got to see Quelch——'

'You'll see him in form—not long now.'

'I mean Wingate! I've got to see Wingate! Think I can keep the captain of the school waiting?'

'Oh, let him wait, along with the Head and Quelch,' said Bob. 'Anybody else that you've got to see? They'll all have to wait!'

'Beast!' roared Bunter.

And he made a rush. Bob Cherry gave him a push on his plump chest, and he tottered back. Then he rushed in another direction, and Vernon-Smith administered a tap to his little fat nose, and he promptly retreated. Another rush brought him into collision with Johnny Bull: and a vigorous shove from Johnny sent him staggering into Squiff, who gave him another shove. He tottered against Peter Todd, who gave yet another shove, and he sat on the ground, with a bump.

'Yaroooh!' roared Bunter, as he sat.

It was that roar that reached the ears of Coker of Fifth, and attracted the attention of the great Horace.

'Ow! Beasts! Wow!' roared Bunter.

'Sit it out, old porpoise!' said Bob Cherry. 'You're not going after those bananas. Sit it out till the bell goes.'

'Beasts!' gasped Bunter. He sat and spluttered for breath.

Grinning faces still surrounded him: there was no escape for the fat Owl. But at that moment, there was a heavy tread under the leafy elms, and a burly figure appeared in the offing. Horace Coker strode on the scene with a knitted brow.

'What's all this?' rapped Coker, in his most magisterial manner. 'Stop this row at once! Do you hear?'

Somehow or other, it always seemed to Horace Coker that he spoke as one having authority, saying 'Do this!' and he doeth it. Coker had what he called a short way with fags. He was prepared to smack their heads as soon as look at them. Sometimes, however, Coker woke up the wrong passengers, so to speak. This time he woke up quite a crowd of wrong passengers. The bunch of Removites turned on him, and most of them spoke at once.

'You cheeky ass, Coker.'

'Mind your own business.'

'Take your face away—if it is a face.'

'Shut up, Coker.'

'Buzz off, fathead!'

'Barge that Fifth-form ass over.'

'Clear off, Coker.'

Coker's rugged face, already wrathy, grew wrathier.

'That does it!' he said. 'If you cheeky little ticks want

your heads smacked all round, I'm the man to smack them. Take that.'

Coker's limerick was crumpled in his left hand. He raised his right, and started the head-smacking process with Bob Cherry. It was a large and heavy hand that suddenly contacted Bob's unlucky head. Smack!

'Take that!' said Coker. 'You butted in this morning, you cheeky young rotter, and—here, hands off—stoppit— oh, my hat!'

Bob tottered, and yelled, as he received that smack. Coker was prepared to go on with the good work. But he had no time. The whole crowd of Removites rushed at him and he was overwhelmed as if by a tidal wave. Bunter, for the moment, was forgotten. All attention was concentrated on Coker.

Coker had a short way with fags. On this occasion, the fags had a short way with Coker. Coker was big and strong, and hefty: but he simply had no chance. In a moment or two, he was up-ended, and he came down on the earth with a bump that almost shook the Greyfriars' quad. The paper flew from his hand, unnoticed, as he rolled and roared. Coker was not thinking of limericks now. He had more pressing matters to think of.

'Bag him!'
'Rag him!'
'Boot him!'
'Bump him!'

Coker surged to his feet, with the juniors grasping him on all sides. They were all too busy to heed Bunter: and the fat Owl made a move to roll away. But alas for Bunter! The whole struggling crowd surged into Bunter as he clambered to his feet, and he rolled over again.

'Ow! wow!' spluttered Bunter. 'Urrrggh! Gerroff! Ooooooh!'

He sat up, dizzily—on Coker's limerick. He sat and gurgled for breath. Wind was always in short supply with Bunter. Now there seemed none at all left in his fat circumference. He gurgled and gurgled.

There was a sudden clang of a bell.

Harry Wharton and Co. in the excitement of dealing with Coker, had rather forgotten class. The clang of the bell reminded them of it.

'Hallo, hallo, hallo, there's the bell!'

'Come on!'

'Good-bye, Coker.'

'Ha, ha, ha!'

Clang! clang! clang! A mob of juniors rushed away at the summons of the bell. But Billy Bunter did not join in the rush. Bunter, winded, still sat and gurgled. Neither did Horace Coker rush. Coker, in a dishevelled and dilapidated state, his collar torn out, his tie gone, his hair a rumpled mop, hardly knowing whether he was on his head or his heels after that brief but hectic affray, stood tottering, gasping for breath, almost as winded as Bunter.

'Oooooogh!' gurgled Bunter.

'Urrrggh!' gasped Coker.

'Wurrrggh!'

'Ooo-er!'

They gurgled and gasped in chorus. And such was the scene that greeted Mr. Prout's eyes, as he came along the path under the elms: and Mr. Prout stopped, in astonishment and wrath, and gazed at that dishevelled and dilapidated member of his form with thunder in his brow.

CHAPTER 8

A SCRAP OF PAPER

'COKER!' boomed Mr. Prout.

'Ooooooh!' gasped Coker.

'Boy!'

'Urrggh! Yes, sir! Oh, crumbs! Yes, sir! Oooh.'

Mr. Prout paid no heed to the fat Owl sitting on the earth and gurgling for wind. He was not concerned with a Remove junior. All his attention was fixed upon the dishevelled and dilapidated member of his own Form. Coker faced him, gasping, and almost tottering. Harry Wharton and Co. had vanished, at the clang of the bell. So why Coker was in that remarkable state was not apparent to his form-master.

'Coker! What does this mean?' boomed Prout. 'You are in a disgraceful state of untidiness. How dare you appear in public in such a state?'

'I—I—I——!' stuttered Coker.

'Disgraceful! Shocking! You are a senior boy, Coker. Have you no sense of the dignity of a senior form?' thundered Prout.

'You see, sir, I—I—I——'

'You have, I presume, been indulging in some unthinking horse-play, like some thoughtless small boy in the Second Form. Have you no sense of decorum, Coker?'

'I—I—I——'

'Go to the House immediately and make yourself tidy, Coker. You should be ashamed of yourself. I am ashamed of you. Your appearance is disgraceful. Go at once.'

'But I—I—I——!'

'Go!' thundered Prout. He raised a plump hand, and pointed. 'Go! I warn you, Coker, that this will not do! More decorous behaviour is expected of a senior boy—a boy in my form—I will not allow boys of my Form to indulge in reckless and unseemly horse-play in the quadrangle. Go!'

Coker, gasping, went.

Mr. Prout stood staring after him, with a thunderous frown, for a moment or two. Then he gave a grunt, expressive of his opinion of Coker, and the state he was in. Then he glanced at Bunter: a glance of disfavour. Then he rolled away with his elephantine tread.

Billy Bunter still sat and gurgled.

The bell had stopped. Other Remove fellows were already in their form-room. Bunter was going to be late for class. But for two or three minutes more, the fat Owl sat and gurgled.

But he heaved himself to his feet at last.

'Beasts!' breathed Bunter. 'No chance at those bananas now—and very likely Quelch won't believe that I never heard the bell! Beasts!'

The fat Owl was about to roll away, when his eyes fell on a crumpled sheet of paper on the ground: revealed now that he was on his feet.

He blinked at it through his big spectacles.

As it lay where he had been sitting, it looked as if he had dropped it there, whatever it was. So he stooped and picked it up, and blinked at it.

Then he stared at it.

'He, he, he!' cachinnated Bunter. 'That's Coker's! It is his fist! He, he, he! He must have dropped it when they collared him. He, he he!'

Chuckling, the fat Owl read:

D

There's a pompous old duffer named Prout,
Enormously podgy and stout,
   He talks awful rot,
   And he never knows what
He is talking and talking about!

Billy Bunter remembered the limerick line he had seen
on the table in Coker's study, and which Bob Cherry had so
thoughtfully obliterated with ink.   Coker, evidently, had
re-started after the interval, and completed that limerick:
and this was it.

'Oh, crikey!' breathed Bunter.   'If old Prout had seen it!
Lucky for Coker that I was sitting on it!   He, he, he!
Right under Prout's nose, if I hadn't sat on it!   He, he, he!
I'll bet Coker will be scared stiff when he remembers it!
He, he, he!'

Billy Bunter blinked round through his spectacles.
Bunter could realize what that remarkable verse would have
meant for Coker, if official eyes had fallen on it.   A fellow
who described his form-master as a pompous old duffer who
did not know what he was talking about, was booked for
disaster of the most disastrous kind.   If Prout's eyes had
fallen on that limerick, scrawled in Coker's unmistakable
hand, he would not have ordered Coker to go and make
himself tidy—he would have walked him off at once to the
headmaster: and there could be little doubt that he would
have demanded that Horace Coker should be expelled from
Greyfriars there and then.   Nor could there be doubt that
Dr. Locke, when he read that limerick, would have acceded
to Prout's demand.   Coker, in fact, had had a narrow
escape of the 'long jump'—owing to the circumstance that
Billy Bunter had been sitting on his limerick while Prout was
in the offing.

Had Coker been still at hand, Bunter would have rolled after him with that limerick, to restore it to safe hands.

But Coker was no longer at hand, and Billy Bunter's blink around revealed no one but his fat self in the deserted quad. Coker had gone into the House several minutes ago, and Prout after him.

'He, he he!' chuckled Bunter. 'I'll bet Coker will be jumpy about this limerick while he's in form! He, he, he! I'll let him have it after class. I'll bet he'll be jolly glad to get it back! He, he, he!'

The fat Owl put the paper into his pocket: and rolled away, at last, to the House.

The Remove were all in form, when he arrived at the form-room. Bunter was five or six minutes late for class: and it was an uneasy Owl that rolled in, under a gimlet-eye that glinted at him. Henry Samuel Quelch was a whale on punctuality: and even one minute's delay was enough to bring a glint to the gimlet-eye.

'Bunter! You are six minutes late!' rumbled Mr. Quelch.

'Oh, yes, sir—no, sir! I—I didn't hear the bell, sir!' In such circumstances, it was Billy Bunter's happy custom to rely on his gifts as an Ananias. 'I—I'm sorry, sir—I—I never heard the bell, sir.'

'Indeed! Have you been out of school bounds, Bunter?' inquired Mr. Quelch.

'Oh! No, sir! Certainly not, sir.'

'If you were within bounds, Bunter, you must have heard the bell. I will not permit unpunctuality in my form——'

'I—I—I mean, some fellows were larking, sir, and I—I was all out of breath when the bell went, sir——'

'Then you did hear the bell, Bunter?'

'Oh! I—I—I mean——'

'You may go to your place, Bunter.'

'Oh! Yes, sir! Thank you, sir.'

'And you will remain in the form-room for half-an-hour after class——'

'Oh, crikey!'

'And write out the conjugation, in both the active and passive voices, of the verb "moneo", Bunter.'

'Oh, lor'!'

The fat Owl gave Harry Wharton and Co. a ferocious blink through his big spectacles, as he rolled to his place. Not only had there been no bananas for Bunter: but he was booked for half-an-hour's detention after class, with nothing but a Latin conjugation to keep him company. And the fact that that would improve his knowledge of the verb 'moneo', in both the active and the passive form, was, to judge by his expression, no comfort at all to Bunter.

CHAPTER 9

CAUGHT BENDING

'BLOW it!'

Coker of the Fifth breathed those words in concentrated tones.

He was looking quite harassed.

Bent almost double, he was scanning the ground, on the spot where his short way with fags had had such a hectic outcome. He was in search of a crumpled sheet of impot paper on which was scrawled the limerick that, as he had told his friends, hit Prout off to a T.

Hitting Prout off to a T was amusing and satisfactory, so far as it went. But it was clear, even to Coker, that if Prout saw the limerick, written in his unmistakable 'fist', the result would be neither amusing nor satisfactory. The result, in fact, would be awful.

Had Coker carried out his masterly plan, of typing that limerick on Mr. Quelch's typewriter, and then carefully destroying the original copy, all would have been well. Typing gave no clue: at any rate, no clue that could lead further than Quelch's study. Prout would have raged: but he would have been left to guess who had described him as a pompous old duffer who talked rot and did not know what he was talking about. And a second typed copy, left on the table in Common-room, for all the Staff to see, would have made him rage more than ever. Prout would have been paid in full for ragging Coker in form, and giving him impots, and then doubling them. And Coker, safely anonymous, would have laughed and enjoyed the whole thing.

But—Coker's masterly plan hadn't been carried out! That limerick, written in a 'fist' that would be known at sight, was scattered somewhere about the Greyfriars' quad. So far from there being no clue to the limericker, anyone who saw that limerick would know that it was Coker's handiwork! And if Prout saw it——!

Coker had nerve. But he almost trembled at that thought. With his mind's eye, he could see himself walked off to the Head for judgment. He could only hope that he would never see it with any other eye!

He had to find that limerick, before anyone else found it.

He had had an hour in form with Prout that afternoon. That hour had been sixty minutes of anxiety, indeed of anguish.

In the excitement of the row with the Removites, he had naturally forgotten all about it. But he had remembered it later. Billy Bunter had foreseen that Coker would be 'jumpy' in form when he remembered it. The hapless Horace was not only jumpy: he was on tenterhooks. He counted the minutes, almost the seconds, till Prout dismissed the Fifth. Then he shot away to the scene of the late shindy, to search for that limerick.

Where was it?

That he had dropped it while grappling with those cheeky fags, was certain. It must be there somewhere. There was little wind: still, it might have blown to some distance. It was not, at all events, to be seen. Bending low, scanning the earth, Coker moved to and fro, concentrated on his search.

'Blow it!' repeated Coker. 'Oh, blow it! Where is the dashed thing? It must be somewhere about here! Blow it!'

Fellows who happened to pass under the elms stared at

Coker, bent double, wondering what he was at. Tubb of the Third came up to inquire. A back-hander from Coker caused George Tubb to depart in a hurry uninformed. Coker was in no mood to be patient with inquisitive fags.

Then Temple, Dabney and Co. of the Fourth, happened along. They stopped to look at Coker.

'What the dooce is that Fifth-form man up to?' asked Temple.

'Looks as if he's looking for something,' said Fry.

'Oh, rather,' said Dabney. 'Lost his wallet perhaps. That man Coker has stacks of money.'

'Might lend him a hand, if that's it!' said Temple. And the three bore down on the searcher.

'Lost something, Coker?' asked Temple.

Coker gave him a glare.

'Yes—get out,' he snapped.

'Like us to help you look for it?'

Coker, in one way, would have been glad of help in searching for that elusive limerick. In another way, help was the last thing he wanted: he did not want other eyes to fall upon such an effusion written in his hand. Very much indeed he did not want that limerick to become the talk of the Lower School, with himself named as author! So instead of accepting that kind offer from Cecil Reginald Temple, he glared at him.

'I said get out!' he bawled.

'Civil, I must say!' remarked Temple, with a sniff.

'Bought the quad, Coker?' asked Fry.

Coker did not reply in words. He had not, certainly, bought the quadrangle: but he acted just as if he had. He charged at the three Fourth-formers, with a large hand smacking at heads.

Temple, Dabney and Co. departed in haste: wishing that

they had not been so obliging. The hefty Horace was too
big to tackle: and they had to be content with telling one
another—at a distance—what they would jolly well have
liked to give Coker for his cheek.

Coker dismissed them from mind, and resumed his vain
search.

Where was that dashed limerick?

Where could it be? Coker, naturally, could not guess
that it was in the pocket of a fat Remove junior who was
detained in his form-room, dismally writing out the conjugation of 'moneo', active and passive. It was about somewhere—it had to be about somewhere—and Coker had to
find it. Bent double again, he scanned and scanned.

'Coker!'

Coker started, and jumped upright. It was Mr. Quelch
this time. Quelch stopped in his walk, looking at Coker:
and Coker had to suppress his feelings. He could not deal
with the Remove master, obviously, as he had dealt with
Tubb of the Third, and Temple and Co. of the Fourth.

'Oh! Yes, sir!' gasped Coker.

'Are you looking for something, Coker?'

'Oh! Yes, sir.'

'Perhaps I can assist you, Coker,' said Mr. Quelch.
'What is it you are looking for?'

Coker was not likely to tell him!

'Oh! I—I—I—a—a—a paper, sir!' he stammered.
'Only a—a—a pip-pip-paper, sir! Don't bother about it,
sir.'

'I will certainly assist you if I can, Coker,' said Mr.
Quelch, benevolently. 'What sort of a paper, Coker?
A Latin exercise?'

'Oh! No! N-n-not a Latin exercise, sir.'

'A letter, perhaps——?'

'Oh! No! N-n-n-not a letter, sir.'

'Well, tell me what it is, and perhaps I may see it,' said
Mr. Quelch: little dreaming how much Coker would have
liked, at that moment, to deal with his majestic 'nut' as he
had dealt with junior heads.

'Only—only a paper, sir,' almost groaned Coker. 'Just
a—a—a paper I—I'd scribbled on, sir. N-not at all
important, sir! Only—only just a scribbled paper, sir!
Just a—a—a scribbled paper——'

'Really, Coker——'

'It—it—it's of no consequence, sir——'

'I quite fail to see, Coker, why you are searching so
assiduously for a scribbled paper of no consequence,'
snapped Mr. Quelch. 'You are an absurd boy, Coker.'

With that, Mr. Quelch walked on: much to Coker's
relief.

'Oh, my hat!' gasped Coker, when Quelch was gone.
'Oh, my only hat! Thank goodness he's gone! Pretty
near as bad for Quelch to see it, as Prout. Oh, crumbs!
I shall be for it, if I don't find that dashed limerick! Where
the dickens can it be?'

Once more bent double, Coker moved on, scanning.
A few minutes later, a deep booming voice caused him to
jump upright again.

'Coker! Upon my word! Coker.'

Coker, resuming the perpendicular, blinked at Mr.
Prout. Prout eyed him with the sternest disapproval.

'Coker! Explain yourself! What are you doing?
What do you mean? Why are you moving about in that
ridiculous manner, bent almost double? Is it your object
to make an absurd exhibition of yourself, Coker?'

'Oh!' gasped Coker. 'No, sir! I—I——'

'Just before class, Coker, I came on you in a dusty,

dishevelled, disreputable state. Now I come on you walking about bent double, in a most absurd and ridiculous attitude. What do you mean by it, Coker?'

'Oh! Nothing, sir! I——'

'I have already warned you, Coker, that a senior boy, in the Fifth Form, is expected to conduct himself with more decorum. I will not allow such antics, Coker! Do you hear me? I will not permit such antics. I warn you very seriously, Coker, that no boy in my form will be permitted to perform such absurd antics! Bear that in mind, Coker.'

Prout, frowning thunderously, rolled on his way.

Coker wiped a spot of perspiration from his heated brow, and gasped for breath.

'Oh, crikey!' he breathed. 'If Old Pompous knew what I was looking for—oh, jiminy!'

It was an appalling thought, that Prout's eyes might have fallen on that limerick. However, 'Old Pompous' fortunately had not the remotest knowledge of that limerick, so far: and Coker hoped fervently that he would remain in that state of blissful ignorance. Coker remained perpendicular until Prout had disappeared: then once more he bent to scan the earth, and the tufts of grass round the elm trees: peering hither and thither, anywhere and everywhere, in search of the lost limerick. Harry Wharton and Bob Cherry, coming along a few minutes later, stopped to stare at him.

'Hallo, hallo, hallo!' murmured Bob. 'This is where Coker's caught bending! What about leap-frog?'

Harry Wharton laughed.

'Coker's asking for it!' he said.

'Come on, then!' grinned Bob. And he rushed. In a moment his hands were on Coker's bent shoulders, and his legs were flying over Coker's bent head. Wharton was only seconds behind him.

'Tuck in your tuppenny, Coker!' yelled Bob, as the captain of the Remove came flying over the astonished Coker.

Wharton was over before Coker quite knew what was happening. He landed and rejoined Bob, as Horace Coker straightened up, spluttering.

'What—what—why, you cheeky fags—you—you—you —jumping over a Fifth-form man's back—why, I—I— I'll——'

Harry Wharton and Bob Cherry, laughing, cut on, and Coker made a fierce stride in pursuit. But he remembered his limerick. That wretched limerick had to be found. And Coker, bottling up his wrath, stooped once more to resume that fruitless search.

CHAPTER 10

LOST LIMERICK

'I SAY, you fellows.'

'Hallo, hallo, hallo! Coming down to the nets, Bunter?'

'Oh, really, Cherry——'

'A spot of cricket would do you good, old fat man.'

'Blow cricket!' said Bunter. 'I say, seen Coker?'

There was a chuckle from the Famous Five. Only a few minutes ago, two members of the Co. had leap-frogged over Coker's back.

'Sort of,' said Bob. 'We caught him bending, and played leap-frog with him. He didn't seem in a good temper about it.'

'Where is he?' asked Bunter.

'You fat villain!' said Harry Wharton. 'Are you thinking of going after those bananas again?'

'Oh, really, Wharton! I haven't been near his study. Besides, Potter and Greene were there, and I couldn't go in.'

'Ha, ha, ha!'

'I want to see Coker,' explained Bunter. 'I've got some-thing of his, and I'll bet he's jolly jumpy about it, too. I was going to give it to him after class, but Quelch kept me in. I shouldn't wonder if he's looking for it now. You see, he dropped a paper when you fellows were ragging him before class, and I picked it up.'

'Oh! I suppose that was why we caught him bending,' said Bob. 'He must have been looking for something, and it was close by where we rolled him over.'

'He jolly well was, and I jolly well know what!' chuckled Billy Bunter. 'I say, look at this, you fellows.'

Billy Bunter groped in a sticky pocket, and disinterred a crumpled sheet of impot paper, with a dusty bullseye adhering to it. That bullseye was immediately transferred to Bunter's mouth. Then the fat Owl held up the paper for the chums of the Remove to read.

'Oh, my hat!' exclaimed Bob. 'That's Coker's fist——'

'It's a limerick!' said Harry. 'Coker's been at it again since you inked that rot in his study. Oh, scissors! If Prout saw that——!'

'There'd be a row,' said Frank Nugent.

'The rowfulness would be terrific!' grinned Hurree Jamset Ram Singh. 'The esteemed and ludicrous Prout would be infuriated.'

'Sack for Coker!' said Johnny Bull. 'Must be a mad ass to write that rubbish and strew it about the quad.'

'Funny, ain't it?' said Bunter, and he proceeded to read the limerick aloud:

'There's a pompous old duffer named Prout,—he, he, he! Enormously podgy and stout,—he, he, he!
    He talks awful rot,
    And he never knows what
He is talking and talking about!—he, he, he!'

'I say, you fellows, fancy Prout's face if he saw that! He, he, he! He'd know Coker's fist at once, of course. Pompous old duffer! He, he, he! Talks awful rot! He, he, he! Would Prout get his hair off? He, he, he!'

'He would jolly well get his hair off—what he's got left,' said Bob. 'For goodness sake, take that back to Coker at once, Bunter. A fellow might be bunked for cheeking his beak like that.'

'He jolly well would,' said Johnny Bull.

'Well, Coker's all sorts of an ass, but we don't want him

bunked,' said Bob. 'Cut off and let Coker have it, Bunter.'

'I'm going to,' said Bunter. 'I'll bet he's got the wind up about it.'

'I'll bet he has! Cut off, and mind you don't lose it.'

'Well, if I take it to him, and he gets it safe back, the least he can do is to ask a fellow to a spread in his study,' said Bunter. Apparently the fat Owl's fat thoughts had been at work, since that limerick had come into his possession. 'What do you fellows think?'

'Fathead!' said Bob. 'Fifth-form men don't ask juniors to spreads in their studies. Not a hope! Just take that silly thing back to Coker, and never mind his spread.'

'Oh, really, Cherry! Think I'm going mooching all over the place looking for Coker, for nothing? But I fancy it will be all right. There must have been lots in that parcel from his Aunt Judy, as well as those bananas. Coker's bound to be jolly glad to get this limerick back, and there's such a thing as gratitude.'

And Billy Bunter, having replaced the limerick in the sticky pocket, rolled on, to look for Coker of the Fifth: leaving the Famous Five laughing. They had no doubt that Coker would be glad to get his limerick back: but they doubted very much whether it would result in a spread in a senior study for the Owl of the Remove.

Bunter, however, hoped for the best, as he rolled on. He grinned as he came in sight of Horace Coker, rooting among the elms. Coker, in a stooping attitude, was moving to and fro, peering into every possible or impossible place for a stray paper. He had to find that paper before somebody picked it up—perhaps a beak!—but the search seemed hopeless, and he was beginning to feel in a state of desperation about it.

'He, he, he!' chuckled Bunter. It seemed quite funny, to

Bunter, for Horace Coker to be searching so frantically for paper that was safe in a sticky pocket.

Coker straightened up, and gave him a deadly glare. Billy Bunter's unmusical cachinnation was, in the circumstances, quite infuriating. Two cheeky Removites had leap-frogged over Coker's back, and escaped unscathed. Now a fat Removite was cackling at him! It was too much.

'Get out!' roared Coker.

'I say, I've come here to——'

'I said get out!' roared Coker.

'All right, but I say, I came here to say—Yaroooh!' roared Bunter, as Coker rushed, and the largest hand in the Greyfriars Fifth established sudden contact with the fattest head in the Remove.

Smack!

'Yaroooh!'

'Now clear off!' roared Coker. 'Want some more! By gum——'

'Yow-ow-ow! Beast! Will you let a fellow speak?' shrieked Bunter. 'I tell you I came here—Whooop!'

Smack!

'Now clear, you fat freak—or——!'

'Ow! wow! Beast! Ow!'

Billy Bunter did not wait to ascertain what would happen to him if he did not clear! He cleared! His little fat legs fairly twinkled as he fled. Coker glared after him, rather regretting that he had not handed out a few more before the fat Owl escaped. Still, smacking Bunter's head made him feel a little better, as he resumed his search for the lost limerick. There was solace in smacking a cheeky fag's head.

Little dreaming that the lost limerick was in the pocket of the fat junior whose head he had smacked, Coker resumed his search.

In such circumstances, he was not likely to find what he sought.

Up and down and round about went Horace Coker, searching and searching: but there was no sign of that limerick. He had to give up the hopeless quest at last: and he wandered away, in an extremely worried and perturbed frame of mind, wondering what the dickens could have become of that limerick, and what on earth would happen if, by awful chance, it came under the eyes of Prout.

CHAPTER 11

A HOT CHASE

BOB CHERRY grinned.

Perhaps it was rather 'cheeky' in a Lower boy to grin, at the sight of Horace James Coker of the Fifth. Undoubtedly it was judicious to keep at a safe distance while grinning at him. Coker really was not a fellow to be grinned at with impunity.

Bob was coming up Friardale Lane from the village. He was sauntering easily with his hands in his pockets. There was plenty of time to get in before 'gates', and it was very pleasant in the country lane, in the sunny summer weather, with the wood on one hand, and the sunny meadows on the other. Bob's cheery face was as sunny as the summer sky: quite a contrast to Horace Coker's, which was dark and clouded and indeed grim. Coker came tramping from the direction of the school, his eyes on the ground, his brow corrugated: trouble written all over his rugged features.

Bob had a kind heart, and could sympathize with any fellow in trouble. But really, Coker seemed to be born to trouble as the sparks fly upward. A fellow who planted eggs in a deck-chair for his form-master to sit on: who composed an outrageous limerick about his beak and left it strewn about the quad, really had to expect a few spots of bother. Wherefore did the sight of Coker's grim and gloomy countenance cause a grin to spread over Bob Cherry's.

Coker looked up, and caught the grin.

His grim brow grew grimmer.

E   59

'You!' he said.

'Little me!' agreed Bob, slowing down to leave a good
space between himself and Coker. He had no use for
Coker's short way with fags. True, smacking Bob's curly
head would not have been so simple a proposition as smacking Billy Bunter's. Bob would have given quite a good
account of himself, even in Coker's mighty grasp. But he
was by no means keen on so disproportionate a combat. It
was necessary to be wary.

'You!' repeated Coker. 'You cheeky, meddling young
pipsqueak——'

'Same to you, and many of them!' said Bob, affably.

The soft answer is said to turn away wrath. But that
answer did not turn away Coker's. Grimmer yet grew his
rugged brow.

The fact was, that Coker was in a perturbed, worried, and
troubled frame of mind, over the disappearance of that
limerick. His temper suffered, in consequence. More and
more clearly, with the lapse of time, Coker had realized how
awful the consequences would be, if that limerick came to
Prout's knowledge. And that might happen at any
moment. The wind, he supposed, must have blown it
somewhere: and anybody might pick it up—Prout himself,
perhaps! Coker, as he tramped down the lane, was trying
to think out that problem: what, in such circumstances, was
a fellow to do? Coker was worried—he was uneasy—he
was apprehensive—and all this added up to an extremely bad
temper. Bob's cheery grin was the last straw. This was
the junior who had, so to speak, come between the wind and
his nobility: the cheeky young rascal who had spoiled his
jape on Prout that morning, and had actually cracked his
own egg on his own Fifth-form nose! Smacking his head,
as he had smacked Bunter's, was naturally the next step.

'You had to butt in, hadn't you, you cheeky little tick,' said Coker. 'Well, now you're getting what you've asked for.'

Coker rushed, with a large hand lifted.

Bob Cherry side-stepped actively, and dodged away. He was certainly not so big and hefty as Coker, but he was a good deal more agile. Twice he dodged Coker's rush, then he leaped lightly up the grassy bank by the side of the lane, ready to dodge into the wood if Coker carried on.

'Keep your wool on, old bean,' he called out, looking down on Coker from that coign of vantage. Coker did not immediately scramble up the steep bank after him. He glared up at him.

'Come down out of that!' commanded Coker.

'Not in these trousers.'

'I'm going to smack your cheeky head!' roared Coker.

'Sez you!' grinned Bob.

Coker glared up. Bob smiled down. That grassy bank was steep, ten or twelve feet up from the lane to the edge of the wood. He was easily out of Coker's reach, unless the Fifth-form man scrambled up the bank after him. That was very probable: and Bob was watchful and wary, prepared to dodge into the wood. Coker was altogether too big and hefty for a Remove junior to handle on his own: if he could help it. The open wood lay behind Bob, with ample space for dodging pursuit. Coker was welcome to chase him, if he liked, under the shady branches, winding among trees and thickets.

Bob, certainly, would have been better pleased, had Coker gone on his way, leaving him to walk back to the school, and tea with the Co. in No. 1 Study. But Coker did not look like going peacefully on his way. His look was expressive, but it expressed anything but peaceful intentions.

'If I come up after you——!' hooted Coker.

'Do!' said Bob.

Coker did! Breathing wrath, Coker charged up the bank.

He charged up with his head down. Bob, from above, reached out with his foot.

He planted that foot, carefully and accurately, on the top of Coker's head as it came within reach, and shoved. He put plenty of force into that shove.

Coker toppled.

'Oh!' gasped Coker. 'Oh! Oooh!'

He made a mighty effort to keep his balance, and failed. He went backwards, rolled down the steep slope, and landed in the lane, with a bump that seemed almost to shake the solid earth. A cloud of dust flew up round him as he landed. He sprawled there, on his back, spluttering.

Then he sat up.

'Ooooooh!' gasped Coker.

The look he cast upward, at the grinning junior at the top of the bank, was positively ferocious. Coker had been in a bad temper to begin with. But that was as moonlight unto sunlight, as water unto wine, compared with his present state of infuriation. He had been on the verge of boiling— now he was boiling over.

For a few moments he sat gasping for breath. Then he scrambled up, covered with the dust of Friardale Lane, and crimson with wrath. Then he started up the grassy bank.

This time he did not charge up head down. He clambered up warily, with gleaming eyes watchfully on Bob.

There was no doubt that, if Coker reached him, Bob Cherry was booked for the time of his life. Sagely, he did not wait for Coker to reach him. There was no chance of tipping Coker over again with a shove from above. Coker

was too watchful for that. So, as Coker came clambering
vengefully up, Bob turned and darted into the wood,
disappearing among the trees.

'Stop!' roared Coker.

Possibly Coker expected the junior to heed that command. But Bob Cherry did not heed. Only a rustle of
thickets came back to Coker.

'By gum!' breathed Coker. 'If I don't smash him—if I
don't spiflicate him—if I don't pulverise him——!'

There were a good many aches and pains in Coker's
sinewy limbs. That bump in the dusty lane had damaged
him a little. Bob was likely to experience a still more
numerous variety of aches and pains, if Coker came within
spiflicating distance. Which Coker was determined to do.
He had forgotten even the lost limerick now, and the peril
that impended from Prout. Only one idea was in Coker's
mind now—to deal faithfully with a junior who had had the
unexampled cheek to tip over a Fifth-form man: and that
Fifth-form man Horace James Coker. Breathing wrath,
Coker charged into Friardale Wood after that junior.

He glimpsed an active figure among the trees.

'Stop!' roared Coker, again.

Again that injunction passed unheeded. Bob cast a
glance back, at a crimson face and a brandished fist: of
which one glimpse was enough for him. He put on speed
and vanished among hawthorns and brambles, with an
exasperated Coker raging after him.

Bob lost no time. There was no time to lose. He ran
hard, winding among the thickets and trees, and the sounds
of pursuit grew fainter behind. But he did not slacken
speed as those sounds died down. Coker, in his present
mood, was a fellow whom it was extremely desirable not to
meet. Bob raced on, with the intention of making a circuit,

and coming out of the wood at another point, leaving Coker to hunt for him as long as he liked. And that simple plan would no doubt have been carried out successfully, had not the unforeseen happened.

It might have occurred to Bob, if he had had time to reflect, that he was not likely to have Friardale Wood all to himself on a summer's afternoon. It was possible, indeed probable, that at least one other person might have sought the hospitable shade of those shady branches. For which reason, there was a spot of recklessness in racing through a wood where the visibility was barred by tangled under-growths.

Bob was not thinking of that, as he raced through a gap in a clump of bushes. He had to think of it a moment later, when he stumbled over a figure reclining in the shade, and came down with a crash on some person unknown, who emitted a startled yell as Bob's weight landed on him fair and square.

CHAPTER 12

MAGNANIMOUS!

MUG PARKISS did not know what was happening to him.

Never had Mug been so completely and utterly taken by surprise.

In that quiet shady glade in Friardale Wood, all was calm and peaceful and reposeful—till Bob Cherry came like a bolt from the blue.

Mug was sprawling in the gass, his head and shoulders resting against a tree-trunk. He was quite at his ease. He was not a pleasant-looking character: indeed on his looks, he was the kind of citizen whom any fellow, not in a tremendous hurry, would have preferred not to meet in a lonely wood. His face, much in need of a wash, was unshaven and bristly. An aroma of tobacco and rum clung to him. His battered hat looked as if it had been picked off a rubbish-heap, his coat was out at the elbows, and his trousers seemed to consist chiefly of patches. Mug was, in fact, a tramp, and on his looks he did not find it a profitable trade.

His bristly face did not express contentment. Mug was not in a good temper. Quite recently Mug had been found suspiciously near a chicken-run, and a farmer, with the assistance of a mastiff, had put Mug to hurried flight. Mug had narrowly escaped leaving some of his patches with the mastiff. Now he was taking a rest after his exertions: and in the shady depths of Friardale Wood, Mug reasonably expected to be able to take his rest undisturbed.

Instead of which, something that seemed like a thunder-bolt, but was in reality a Greyfriars' junior, came whizzing through a gap in the bushes close by Mug, stumbled over him, and landed on him, crashing.

'Oh!' gasped Bob Cherry.

'Oooogh!' spluttered Mug.

Bob sprawled over him, almost winded by the shock. Mug, quite winded, sprawled under Bob, spluttering and gurgling.

'Urrrggh! Wot's that? Oo's that? Gerroff!' gurgled Mug.

'Oh, my hat!'

Bob scrambled off the tramp. Mug sat up, gasping for breath. As he realized that it was this schoolboy who had crashed on him and flattened him out, the glare that he gave Bob was quite alarming. Mug was rather hurt—that, in the circumstances, was unavoidable. He was more enraged than hurt, however.

'You—you——!' gurgled Mug.

'Oh! Sorry!' gasped Bob, 'I didn't see you—never knew anybody was about here—I'm awfully sorry, really. I—I hope you're not hurt.'

As he spoke, Bob glanced back, and listened. A rustling came from afar. It indicated a pursuing Coker. But it was not close at hand. And Bob really was concerned about the person upon whom he had crashed, unintentionally, but very heavily.

'Urt!' repeated Mug. 'Think you can bang down on a bloke without 'urting him, you young idjit? Blow me tight! 'Urt, says you! You young lunatic, I'm 'urt, and you're going to be 'urt too, you can lay to that.'

Mug scrambled to his feet.

Bob backed away promptly. He realized that this squat, thickset fellow was more dangerous than Coker, at close quarters. But Mug came at him with a spring like that of a tiger. Bob, still backing, put up his hands in defence.

'Look here, I'm sorry,' he said, 'I never saw you—Keep off, will you?'

'Praps you'll look where you're running, another time!' yapped Mug. 'Praps you think you can knock a man flat, and wallop down on 'im, because he's in 'ard luck. You got it coming, you young 'ound.'

Two grimy fists that looked like legs of mutton lashed at Bob. Mug was in an evil temper. Quite a good-tempered man might have been annoyed by what had happened: and Mug Parkiss was far from being a good-tempered man. He was in a mood to give any victim who came his way, what he would have liked to give that farmer and his mastiff. And head-smacking, on Coker's lines, was not Mug's idea at all. He came at the schoolboy hitting out savagely, as he was wont to hit when engaged in a shindy at a 'pub'.

Bob, sturdy as he was, had no chance at all. The thick-set tramp had twice his weight and twice his strength. Defending himself as well as he could, he backed and backed under Mug's onslaught, till his foot caught in a trailing bramble, and he went over on his back.

'Got cher!' hissed Mug.

And he fairly threw himself on Bob, hitting hard and often.

'Help!' yelled Bob, at the top of his voice, as he struggled frantically under that attack. 'Help!'

'Oo's goin' to 'elp yer!' snarled Mug. 'Take that, and that, and that!'

'Help!' shrieked Bob, struggling frantically.

He could only hope that somebody might be in the wood, and might hear him. Even Coker would have been welcome at that moment.

He yelled and yelled, as Mug thumped and thumped.

There was a rustle in the bushes. Horace Coker had lost Bob's track in the wood. But he was well within hearing of those desperate shouts.

Coker came through the bushes almost at a gallop.

'What the dickens——!' exclaimed Coker, blankly He halted, staring at the scene that met his eyes.

Coker had been on the trail of vengeance. It had been his fell intention to give that cheeky junior the whopping of his life—if he caught him. Now that cheeky junior was caught: but the sight of a Greyfriars' junior struggling and squirming under a savage attack from a ruffianly tramp, quite changed the current of Coker's ideas.

For a moment he stared, blankly. Then he rushed. He grasped the back of Mug's frowsy neck, and dragged him by main force from the panting schoolboy.

'You rotter!' roared Coker.

'Oh, crumbs!' gasped Bob. He sat up, dizzy, breathless. 'Look out, Coker—look out for that brute!'

Mug Parkiss went spinning as Coker flung him away. But he recovered his balance in a moment, and came at Coker, with leg-of-mutton fists in action.

'Look out!' panted Bob.

But Coker was looking out. His own fists, almost as hefty as Mug's, were up: and his rugged face was grim. He met Mug with right and left. A knuckly fist crashed on his chest, and another on his face. Coker hardly blinked. His own punches landed still harder—one in Mug's eye, and the other on his nose. Mug went staggering back.

'Oh! Good man!' gasped Bob.

'You rotter!' roared Coker. 'Come on, if you want some more!'

Mug apparently, did want some more, for he came on

again, his bristly face flaming. Coker stood up to him
without a sign of flinching. Coker had little science: as a
boxer he did not shine: but he had a tremendous punch.
His punches landed on Mug like the kicks of a mule.
Punches came back, but Coker gave more than he received,
and he gave them harder.

Bob watched breathlessly.

Few schoolboys could have stood up to Mug. The
hefty Horace was one of the few. He not only stood up to
Mug but he knocked him right and left. Coker received
some hard knocks: but he seemed hardly conscious of them.
He was concentrated on giving Mug still harder ones.
Coker had unlimited pluck: but there was a yellow streak
in Mug. After a few minutes of it, he was backing away—
and as Coker followed him up, still delivering tremendous
punches, Mug suddenly took to his heels, and ran.

'Had enough?' roared Coker.

There was no reply from Mug: but clearly he had had
enough. Only a rustle of the thickets came back, as he
vanished into the wood.

Coker stood panting. He dabbed a perspiring face
with a handkerchief. One of his eyes was winking a little:
and there was a thin red streak from his nose. He dabbed
and dabbed.

While he dabbed, he frowned at Bob.

'You cheeky young tick!' he said.

Bob scrambled to his feet—with a wary eye on Coker.
Coker, in those hectic moments, had been more than
welcome: never, in fact, had Bob been so glad to see any
Greyfriars' fellow, as he had been to see Coker arrive on the
spot. But he had to be wary. Having rescued him from
the tramp, it would have been quite like Coker to carry on
with his original intention of administering a whopping.

HIS PUNCHES LANDED ON MUG LIKE THE KICKS OF A MULE.

Bob was grateful for his rescue: but he did not want the whopping.

'I say, thanks, Coker,' he ventured. 'I say, I should have been knocked black and blue by that brute, if you hadn't come up. It was jolly decent of you to barge in, Coker, old chap.'

Coker stared at him.

'Don't be a young ass!' he said.

'Eh?'

'Think I was going to let a tramp knock a kid about?' snapped Coker. 'And don't call me old chap. I don't like, it from fags.'

Bob grinned. Coker had saved him from a terrific hammering: but Coker was still Coker!

'And don't grin at me!' added Coker, sternly. 'I don't allow cheeky fags to grin when I'm speaking to them.'

Bob assumed as serious an expression as he could.

'Well, thanks,' he said. 'And I'm sorry I up-ended you in the lane, too.'

Coker gave him a cold stare.

'You didn't up-end me in the lane,' he snapped.

'Eh?'

'My foot slipped——'

'Oh!'

'I'd like to see a Remove fag up-end me,' said Coker. 'Don't be a silly young idiot, Cherry, if you can help it.' Coker dabbed trickling red from his nose. 'I was going to give you a thrashing, Cherry, and I've a jolly good mind to now—but you look as if you've had enough from that rough.'

'Quite enough,' agreed Bob. 'A little too much, really.'

'Well, I'll leave it at that,' said Coker, magnanimously. 'But you'd better take care not to cheek me again, Cherry.

I've a short way with fags, I can tell you. I don't stand any cheek. Keep that in mind.'

'I will,' said Bob, meekly. It was no time to tell Coker what he thought of him. Coker, for the time being at least, was welcome to throw his weight about, all over the county of Kent, so far as Bob was concerned.

'Well, that's all right,' said Coker, almost graciously. 'Now I'd better see you safe out of the wood, in case that ruffian's still hanging about.'

'Oh, I shall be all right——'

'Don't answer back,' said Coker. 'I've said I'm going to see you safe out of this wood. No need for you to say anything.'

Bob Cherry breathed rather hard. But he was too grateful to Coker for rescue, to retort as he would have retorted in other circumstances.

'Just as you like, Coker,' he said, with quite unaccustomed meekness.

'Of course it's as I like,' said Coker. 'I know best, I suppose! Just shut up and come along with me.'

Bob Cherry obediently shut up and came along. He walked back to Friardale Lane with Coker, who dabbed and dabbed his nose as he went. In the lane, Coker dismissed him with a gesture, as the Great Panjandrum might have dismissed some very small and inconsiderable person. And Bob Cherry headed once more for Greyfriars and did not chuckle till he was out of Coker's hearing.

CHAPTER 13

WHISTLE FOR IT!

'BETTER wait for Coker, I suppose!' said Potter.

'Better, I suppose,' assented Greene.

'Why the dickens doesn't he come up?'

'Oh, I expect he's still looking for that limerick of his. Just like Coker to strew it about in the quad, wasn't it?'

'Oh, just!'

Potter and Greene were in their study, in the Fifth. They were ready for tea, as fellows naturally were when it was past tea-time.

They had disinterred ample supplies from the study cupboard. There was, as Billy Bunter had sagely surmised, much more in the parcel from Aunt Judy than those bananas. Quite an attractive spread adorned the study table. Potter and Greene were very much disposed to begin on it. Still, they felt that they had to wait till Horace Coker blew in. After all, it was Coker's spread.

So they waited—not patiently.

Often and often, they were not at all keen to see Coker. But at such a time as this, naturally they wanted to.

In a way, they rather liked old Horace. No doubt he was rather aggressive, rather over-bearing, rather given to laying down the law, and regarding conversation as a one-way traffic. But he had his good points—in fact he had many good points, for his parcels from Aunt Judy were numerous.

But though they did really like old Horace, in a way, they found him very trying at times. This was one of the times:

for they were hungry, and wanted their tea, and Coker had not come up to the study. And they felt that they really couldn't begin on Coker's spread without Coker.

The last they had seen of him, he had been in the quad, searching for that lost limerick. That had been a considerable time ago. Whether he was still searching for that limerick, or whether he had given up the quest, they did not know. Nor would they have cared to know, had it not been tea-time, and past. They waited—impatiently: Greene helping himself from a box of figs to go on with.

'The ass!' said Potter. 'Awful ass to write that idiotic limerick at all. But was it any use telling him so?'

'Hardly,' sighed Greene. 'Have some of these figs, old chap.'

Potter had some.

'He was going to type it out on Quelch's typewriter,' resumed Potter. 'Ten to one Quelch would have walked in and caught him at it.'

'A hundred to one,' said Greene.

'And if Quelch hadn't, Prout would have copped him, putting it on his study table for him.'

'Bound to have,' agreed Greene.

'And this isn't just a silly fag trick, like putting an egg in his deck-chair for old Pompous to sit on. Chap might be sacked for this.'

'Jolly likely.'

'And then he has to go and get mixed up in a shindy with a mob of fags, and leave it strewn about the quad! Not typed, mark you—but in his own fist, that old Pompous knows as well as he knows his own. If Prout happened to pick it up——!'

'And he might! Anybody might! Coker all over!'

'Of all the chumps——!' said Potter.

'Of all the dithering fatheads——!' said Greene.

'Of all the nitwits——!' said Potter.

'Of all the silly cuckoos——!' said Greene.

'Of all the blithering boobies——!' went on Potter. But he was interrupted by a tramp of heavy feet, and Horace Coker came into the study. Potter stopped his remarks quite suddenly.

'Oh, here you are,' said Coker. 'What's that—who's a blithering booby, Potter? Talking about Prout?'

'Oh! Ah! Exactly!' gasped Potter.

'Well, better not let him hear you,' said Coker. 'Might come nosing into the study again, after my impot.'

'Haven't you done it?' asked Greene.

'Don't be an ass, Greeney. Have I had time to write lines, when I've been hunting for that dashed limerick?' snapped Coker.

'Found it yet?'

'Not yet. I've got to find it, though.' Coker gave his nose a rub. Both Potter and Greene were looking rather curiously at that nose. Coker had had no time to write lines: but it seemed that he had had time to get into a scrap of some sort.

'Been in a row?' asked Potter.

'Oh, no! Nothing much,' said Coker. 'I thrashed a tramp down the lane, that's all. He got in one or two before he had enough—nothing much. I had one on the boko. Does it show much?'

'A bit like a beetroot,' said Potter, surveying it.

'More like a tomato, I think,' said Greene.

Coker grunted and walked across to the looking-glass, and surveyed his features therein. Behind his broad back, Potter winked at Greene. Neither of Coker's pals was surprised to hear that he had been in a row. Coker was oftener in a row than out of one. They grinned: rather forgetful of the fact that their faces were reflected in the glass as well as Coker's.

'What are you fellows grinning at?' demanded Coker, turning round.

'Oh! Nothing,' said Potter, hastily.

'Nothing at all,' said Greene.

'Well, don't grin like a pair of hyenas at nothing,' said Coker. 'If you think it funny for a fellow to get a jolt on the boko——'

'Not at all, old chap! I wonder what's become of that limerick,' said Potter, judiciously changing the subject. 'I suppose you looked everywhere for it.'

'Jolly nearly everywhere,' said Coker. 'Must have blown away, I suppose, and goodness knows where. It's a worry, you men,' said Coker, gloomily. 'If old Pompous saw it, he would go right off at the deep end. He would just hate being called a pompous old duffer who talks rot, and doesn't know what he is talking about.'

'Not the sort of thing a beak would like,' agreed Potter.

'It's true, of course,' said Coker. 'Prout is a pompous old duffer, and he talks awful rot—you heard him, in the form-room this morning, when he made out that I'd skewed in con. He jolly well doesn't know what he's talking about, just as I put it in my limerick. But——' Coker shook his head. 'You can't tell a beak that, you know. There'll be a fearful row if Prout sees that limerick.'

'There will!' agreed Potter and Greene.

'All right if I'd typed it out and left it on his table for him. But you see, that limerick's in my fist. Anyone who found it would know that I'd done it. I've simply got to find it. I can't have it hanging over my head like this, like the sword of Sophocles——'

'The sword of whom?' ejaculated Potter.

'Sophocles!' snapped Coker. 'Chap who had a sword hanging over his head by a bit of twine, or something——'

'Oh! Damocles!' said Potter. 'You mean the sword of Damocles.'

Coker gave him a look.

'I said the sword of Sophocles, and I mean the sword of Sophocles,' he answered. 'If you want to show off your ignorance, Potter, you can keep it for Prout in the form-room. He likes it! Look at the fuss he made this morning, when he had Virgil wrong, and I had it right! Keep it for him, old chap, and don't argue with a fellow who knows. What are you grinning at, Greene?'

'Oh! Nothing,' said Greene. 'What about tea?'

'May as well,' said Coker. 'We're a bit late. I'll have another hunt for that dashed limerick after tea, and you fellows can come and help me. I've got to find that limerick, if I have to go over the whole quad with a small comb. Now let's have tea.'

They sat down to tea.

That meal was still in progress, when the study door opened, without a knock. The three Fifth-form men glanced round at a fat face, adorned by a big pair of spectacles, looking in.

Coker gave that fat face a glare.

'You fat freak, what do you want here?' he exclaimed. 'Get out.'

Billy Bunter did not come in. He stood in the doorway, a fat hand holding the door-handle, ready to slam the door if—or rather when—hostilities accrued. He blinked at Horace Coker with a devastating blink.

'Yah!' was his first remark.

'Want me to smack your silly head again?' demanded Coker.

'Beast! You won't find that limerick!'

Coker started.

'That limerick! What do you know about my limerick?' he exclaimed. So far as Coker was aware, the existence of that limerick was known only to himself and Potter and Greene. It was quite startling to learn that news of it had reached the Remove.

'He, he, he! I know all about it, Coker! You see, I picked it up,' chuckled Bunter.

'You've picked up my limerick?' gasped Coker. 'Oh! Good! Hand it to me, you fat tick! Sharp.'

'Yah! You jolly well smacked my head, when I looked for you to give it to you, you beast! Now you can jolly well whistle for it, see?'

'Hand it over at once!' roared Coker.

'Yah!'

'By gum, I'll jolly well——' Coker jumped up.

Slam!

Billy Bunter slammed the door shut. A rapid patter of feet echoed back from the passage.

Evidently, Bunter had not come there to hand over that limerick. Smacking Bunter's fat head had, apparently, changed his intentions. Once more, Coker's short way with fags had been his undoing! Billy Bunter had looked in, not to hand over the limerick, but to tell Coker to whistle for it! Having told him, he fled for his fat life.

'Oh, my hat!' said Potter. 'If that fag's got your limerick, Coker, he will show it all over the school.'

'It will get to Prout!' breathed Greene.

'After him!' panted Coker. 'Collar him and get it

back! Come on.' Coker wrenched open the door, and rushed in pursuit.

Potter and Greene exchanged a glance. Sad to relate, they were more interested in Coker's spread than in Coker's limerick.

'Feel like chasing a fag all over the shop, Greeney?' asked Potter.

'Not a lot!' said Greene. 'I'd rather finish my tea.'

'Same here!' concurred Potter.

And they went on with their tea.

Coker, regardless of tea in such circumstances, raced down the passage after Bunter. Billy Bunter, putting on uncommon speed, had reached the landing. Remove fellows were coming up to the studies to tea, and there were six or seven of them on the landing, Vernon-Smith, Redwing, Peter Todd, Squiff, Tom Brown, Lord Mauleverer, all stared at the fat Owl, as he came bolting breathlessly from the Fifth-form studies.

'I say, you fellows!' gasped Bunter. 'I say—rescue—Yaroooh!' Coker came up with a rush and a large hand swiped. Smack!

'Now, then——!' panted Coker.

'Ow! Leggo! Help!' yelled Bunter.

The large hand rose and fell again.

Smack!

'Yooo-hooop!'

'Now, you fat freak—Stop!' roared Coker, as Bunter charged through the crowd of staring Removites on the landing.

He charged in pursuit.

Bunter got through. But Coker did not: for Herbert Vernon-Smith and Peter Todd, simultaneously, each put a foot in Coker's way. Coker, tripped, measured his length on the landing, with a bump and a roar.

Billy Bunter flew down the staircase.

By the time a breathless and enraged Coker scrambled to his feet, and renewed the pursuit, Bunter had vanished. And he sagely stayed vanished.

CHAPTER 14

AFTER LIGHTS OUT

'BOTHER!' mumbled Bob Cherry.

He turned his head on his pillow.

'Blow!'

He turned it again.

The cheery Bob did not often make grousing remarks. And probably it was the first time that he had made one at midnight. At midnight's stilly hour, Bob's eyes were, as a rule, closed in the sound slumber of healthy youth.

But for once, Bob was not asleep when the chime of twelve came from the old clock-tower. Everyone else in the Remove dormitory was slumbering. A deep and resonant snore told that Billy Bunter was fast bound in slumber's chain. Bob was the only fellow awake. It was unusual, and it was uncomfortable, wherefore did Bob mumble 'Bother' and 'Blow'.

The hefty thumps administered by Mug Parkiss, in Friardale Wood, that afternoon, were the cause. Mug had thumped hard, and he had thumped often, before Coker had arrived to the rescue. Bob was not the fellow to make a fuss about a few hard knocks. Neither did he make a fuss. But a variety of aches and pains liberally distributed over him, did not make for repose. Lingering pangs and twinges, like Macbeth, murdered sleep. Generally, when his eyes closed on his pillow, they did not open again till the rising-bell clanged in the dewy morn. Now he had only a series of cat-naps, and awoke again and again from uneasy slumber: and midnight found him wide awake.

It was in vain that he counted sheep jumping over a stile. Innumerable sheep jumped over that stile and left him still wakeful. He was tempted to wake one of his friends, just to hear a voice to break the monotony. Willingly he would have sat up in bed and discussed the forthcoming match at St. Jim's, with Harry Wharton or Frank Nugent or Johnny Bull or the nabob of Bhanipur. But that would have been rather selfish, and he refrained: if he couldn't sleep, that was no reason why other fellows shouldn't.

But it was dismal, sleepless, staring at the glimmering starlight at the high windows of the dormitory. He could have envied Billy Bunter, whose steady snore went on and on, like the unending melody in Wagnerian music, though considerably less musical.

'Blow,' mumbled Bob. 'Blow that tramp, and blow that fathead Coker. Blow.'

Bob was grateful to Horace Coker for rescuing him from the tramp. But it was Coker's fault that he had run into that tramp at all. So he 'blowed' both of them impartially.

Wearily, he settled his head on the pillow once more, in the hope of wooing balmy slumber. But slumber came not. Something else, to his surprise, did come—a sound in the silence that revealed that the dormitory door had opened.

Bob gave quite a jump, and raised his head from the pillow.

It was past midnight, he knew: he had heard the succession of strokes from the clock-tower. At that time of night, all Greyfriars slept—or should have slept. The last light had been extinguished—the last door closed. Breakers of bounds, after lights out, were not absolutely unknown: but the most reckless breaker of bounds would hardly keep it up so late as this. It was simply astonishing for the door of the Remove dormitory to open at such an hour.

'That ass Smithy!' breathed Bob.

The door had opened: that was certain. In the deep silence, he could detect a soft and stealthy tread. Late as it was, he concluded that it must be Smithy—the reckless manners and customs of the 'Bounder' were well known in the Remove. It could only be Herbert Vernon-Smith, returning late from some reckless excursion out of bounds.

But the next moment, Bob knew that it was not Smithy.

In the starlight that streamed in at the high windows, his eyes picked up a much taller figure than Smithy's.

Bob stared blankly at that figure.

It was not Smithy's. It was a head taller than Smithy's. Smithy was in bed, fast asleep like the rest. It was not a member of the Remove who had come into the dormitory. Who, and why, was quite a mystery—till a glimmer of the starlight fell on a rugged face.

'Coker!' breathed Bob.

He sat up, staring.

It was Horace Coker, of the Fifth Form!

Bob stared amazed. 'Dormitory raids' sometimes occurred, among the juniors. Temple, Dabney and Co. of the Fourth, might have raided the Remove dormitory—or the Remove might have raided the Fourth. But the Fifth, a senior form, were above such pranks. It was simply amazing to see a Fifth-form man tiptoeing into a junior dormitory at the witching hour of night.

But there was no doubt that it was Horace Coker. The summer starlight showed up his rugged features, and glimmered on a nose still red and rather raw from Mug Parkiss's knuckles.

Coker had tiptoed in. Had all the Remove been asleep, no ear could have heard a sound. Whatever Coker's object in paying that extraordinary nocturnal visit, he would have

carried on undisturbed, but for the effect of Mug's knuckles
on Bob Cherry.

Bob's grasp closed on his pillow. His natural impulse
was to hurl that pillow at the nocturnal intruder.

But he remembered the rescue that afternoon. Coker
had done him a good turn. The aches and pains that
lingered in his sturdy frame would certainly have been
increased and multiplied, but for Coker's intervention. He
left that pillow where it was.

Coker was standing in the starlight, his head bent a
little, as if to listen. The only sound audible in the
dormitory was the snore of Billy Bunter. As if that snore
was the guide he wanted, Coker moved in the direction of
Billy Bunter's bed.

Bob's amazed stare followed him.

He halted at Bunter's bed, and bent his head to stare at
the sleeper. The glimmering starlight was enough to reveal
the fat Owl's fat features. Coker straightened up again,
as if satisfied.

He turned to a chair beside the bed. On that chair
sprawled Bunter's clothes. They were not neatly folded.
Billy Bunter did not believe in taking unnecessary trouble.
His garments sprawled anyhow over the chair.

Coker grasped at them.

'Oh, crumbs!' breathed Bob.

Amazing as it was in a Fifth-form senior, especially
amazing in a senior with so lofty a sense of his own dignity
and importance as Horace Coker, he was there for a 'lark',
just like some thoughtless junior! He was going to lark
with a fellow's clothes!

So, at any rate, it could only seem to Bob Cherry. That
Coker of the Fifth was after a crumpled document in a sticky
pocket naturally did not occur to him. He had forgotten

all about Coker's limerick: and if he had remembered it, he would have supposed that Bunter had handed it to Coker, as he had intended to do.

But Coker was, in fact, after that limerick.

Billy Bunter had told him to 'whistle' for it: but obviously whistling for it was not the way to recover it. Since then the fat Owl had successfully dodged an encounter with Coker.

Hence that nocturnal visit to the Remove dormitory that so amazed Bob Cherry. Coker had thought it out. Thinking was not much in Coker's line: but the awful peril of Prout seeing that limerick spurred Coker's rather solid brain into unusual activity. Having thought it out, it looked easy to Coker. Easy enough to go through the little fat tick's pockets while he was asleep, and extract that limerick. So there was Coker, after his limerick.

Had Bob Cherry been aware of the object of Coker's visit, he would not have thought of intervening, to prevent Horace from recovering possession of his own property. But Bob had not the remotest idea why Coker was there. All he knew was, that a Fifth-form man had tiptoed into the Remove dormitory at midnight, and was grabbing up the clothes of a slumbering Removite.

Taking away a fellow's clothes, or hiding them, while he was asleep, was a fag trick, of which he would never have dreamed Coker capable. But there was Coker, under his eyes in the starlight, doing that very thing!—larking with Bunter's clothes while Bunter snored!

Bob's grasp closed again on his pillow. No Fifth-form man was getting away with such a lark in Remove territory!

Whiz!

The pillow flew with accurate aim.

Coker did not know what was coming, and he hardly

knew what it was when it came. All he knew was that
something came like a bolt out of the blue, smote his head,
curled round it, and hurled him over sprawling across Billy
Bunter's bed—and Billy Bunter.

'Oh!' gasped Coker. 'Oh! What—Oh! Oh!'

'Yaroooh!' came a roar from a suddenly-awakened
sleeper.

Billy Bunter was not easy to wake. But a Fifth-form
man sprawling suddenly over him effectually awakened
Bunter. He roared, and wriggled under unexpected weight.

No more than Coker did the fat Owl know what was
happening. It seemed to him that the ancient roof of
Greyfriars had fallen in. Something very heavy was
squashing him.

'Yaroooh! Ooooooh! What's that? Help!' yelled
Bunter.

'Oh, scissors!' gasped Coker.

'Yooo-hooop! Help! I say, you fellows, the roof's
fallen in!' yelled Bunter. 'I say, help! Oh, crikey!
Yooo hooop!'

'Ha, ha, ha!' came a roar from Bob Cherry.

A dozen voices became audible at once. The Remove
had been sound asleep. But that sudden uproar would have
awakened Rip van Winkle.

'What's up?'

'Who's that?'

'What the thump——'

'What the terrific dickens——'

Coker struggled off Bunter's bed, dizzily. Bunter's
garments, which he had grabbed, had fallen from his grasp,
and were strewn over the bed and the floor.

He did not seek to recover them. Even Coker realized
that the game was up, with every fellow in the dormitory

wide awake: all exclaiming, and some turning out of bed, and Bunter's yells waking the echoes. Prompt retreat was indicated.

'I say, you fellows, help!' roared Bunter. 'I say—— Something fell on me—I say, the roof's falling in——'

'Shut up, you fat ass!' hooted Bob. It's only Coker——'

'Coker!' exclaimed Harry Wharton.

'Yes, Coker—larking in the dorm! I got him with my pillow—there he goes——!' Bob pointed to a hurried figure flitting doorward in the starlight.

'Coker—that Fifth-form ass——'

'Collar him!'

'Coker—in the middle of the night! By gum! Bag him!'

'Scrag him!'

'That fathead Coker——'

'That terrific ass Coker——'

Coker dashed for the door. Prompt retreat was Coker's cue, with the Remove buzzing round him like a hive of angry bees. Only Vernon-Smith was in time to give Coker a parting shot. The Bounder was quick on the uptake, and quick off the mark. His pillow followed Coker to the door, and caught him in the back of the neck.

'Wooooooh!' came a howl from Coker, as he nose-dived through the doorway, under the propulsion of the whizzing pillow.

'Got him!' chuckled Smithy.

Bumps sounded from the passage. Then there was a sound of hasty hurried footsteps. Coker was gone.

He left the Remove dormitory in an excited buzz. Billy Bunter, realizing at last that the roof had not, after all, collapsed on him, ceased to roar. But he gave a startled squeak, as he heard Bob Cherry explaining——

'The silly ass came here larking—he was larking with Bunter's clobber. Fancy a Fifth-form man—larking with a fellow's clobber like a silly fag in the Second! I jolly well stopped him with my pillow——'

'Oh, crikey!' breathed Bunter.

A Fifth-form man, larking with a fellow's clobber after lights out, was a surprise to the juniors. Coker, they knew, was every imaginable kind of silly ass: but this was the limit, even for Coker! But Billy Bunter knew better—he could guess why Coker had come. And he rolled out of bed and gathered up his clobber, and groped in a sticky pocket to make sure that a crumpled document was there. And while the other fellows discussed that latest example of Horace Coker's extraordinary fatheadedness, Billy Bunter tucked that crumpled document under his pillow: where, under his fat head, he had no doubt that it would be safe till morning. And his first proceeding after rising-bell in the morning, was to find a safer hiding-place for it in his study.

CHAPTER 15

ON TENTERHOOKS

'He, he, he!'

Harry Wharton and Co. glanced round.

It was the following morning, in break. Bright sunshine streamed down on the old quadrangle of Greyfriars. The Famous Five were sauntering by the elms, talking cricket. The fixture with St. Jim's was a matter of much interest to them: while Billy Bunter, on the other hand, was not interested at all. Nevertheless, they glanced round, as the fat Owl's unmusical chortle fell on their ears.

Billy Bunter was grinning all over his fat face, his eyes and spectacles fixed on a burly figure that had emerged from the House.

The sight of Horace Coker, that sunny morning, seemed to entertain Bunter—and none the less because Coker's brow was knitted grimly, indicating that he was in a truculent mood.

Coker, sighting Bunter, bore down on him at once. The fattest face in the Remove might have been expected to register alarm.

But it did not! Only too clearly, the burly Fifth-form man was bearing down on him with hostile intent. But there was no sign of alarm in Billy Bunter's plump countenance. He grinned at Coker.

'Look out, fatty,' called out Bob Cherry. 'Coker's on your track.'

'What do I care?' retorted Bunter, disdainfully.

'Have you been snooping in his study again?' asked

Harry Wharton. 'If you have, you'd better cut, you fat ass.'

Billy Bunter sniffed.

'Catch me cutting!' he answered. 'Who's Coker, I'd like to know? Coker had better mind his ps and qs, I can tell you.'

At which the chums of the Remove could only stare.

Coker was too hefty a proposition for even one of their own select circle to handle. Bunter would have folded up in his grasp, as helpless in that grasp as a fat rabbit in the coils of a boa-constrictor. And Bunter, assuredly, was not of the stuff of which heroes are made. Bunter had been known to dodge round corners to elude Tubb of the Third. So it was quite astonishing to see him facing up to Coker in his wrath, with a grinning fat face, and without turning a hair.

Coker came striding up, brows knitted and eyes glinting. His nocturnal adventure, or rather misadventure, in the Remove dormitory, had not improved Coker's temper. Coker, that morning, was rather like a bear with a sore head. He had found it hard, very hard, to keep patience with Prout in early school. Prout, in form, had been irritating as usual. He had even found fault with Coker for spelling 'mixture' 'micksture': which, as Coker told Potter and Greene, was pretty near the limit, even for Prout. Altogether, Horace Coker was quite a dangerous character for Billy Bunter to meet in break. Yet the fat Owl merely grinned.

Coker gave no heed to the Famous Five. He concentrated on Bunter. The look he gave him was petrifying. Bunter, however, seemed completely unpetrified.

'Now I've got you, you little fat tick!' said Coker, grimly. 'You were dodging me yesterday, you little fat flabby footling freak, but I've jolly well got you now.'

'Want anything, Coker?' asked Bunter, with a calmness that was quite amazing to the Famous Five, looking on.

'I want my limerick, you little fat smudge. Hand it over before I smack your cheeky head!'

'You smack my head, and see what's coming to you!' retorted Bunter, coolly. 'Want Prout to see that limerick? He's jolly well going to see it, if you start throwing your weight about, Coker.'

'I fancy not!' said Coker. 'If you don't hand it over this minute, you fat porker, I'll collar you and go through your pockets for it, see!'

Harry Wharton and Co. exchanged glances. It was news to them that Coker's limerick was still in Bunter's possession.

'Like to go through my pockets, Coker?' grinned Bunter. 'Like you were going to last night in the dorm, what? He, he, he!'

'Oh!' murmured Bob Cherry.

'Go ahead, if you like,' added Bunter. 'You wouldn't find it, Coker. Not after last night—he, he, he! I've shoved it in a safe place, see? You jolly well smack my head, Coker! I'll jolly well fish it out and walk it off to Prout! Go it!'

A large hand was already raised. But it did not land on Billy Bunter's fat head. Slowly, but inevitably, it dropped to Coker's side again.

Bunter had told him to 'go it'. But Coker did not 'go it'. It dawned on his powerful brain that Bunter, warned by last night's happenings, had taken precautions. Bunter couldn't go on dodging Coker for ever: but the simple expedient of hiding that limerick in a safe place made further dodging unnecessary.

Billy Bunter was quite prepared to face Coker in his

G

wrath, now that that document was no longer in a sticky
pocket.

'Where is it?' gasped Coker.

'Find out!' retorted Bunter, independently.

'I—I—I'll spiflicate you—I—I—I'll——'

'Oh, do!' said Bunter, airily. 'I fancy you'll feel a bit
spiflicated yourself, when Prout sees that limerick. Pompous old duffer! He, he, he!'

'You—you—you——!' gasped Coker.

The large hand was raised again. Barely could Coker
restrain himself from landing it on the grinning fat Owl.
Never had he so longed and yearned to smack any fellow's
head: and he was not accustomed to restrain such longings
and yearnings. Very, very nearly did he smite. But not
quite! Billy Bunter's fat head, only a yard away, was as
safe as if it had been a hundred miles distant. Bunter had
the whip-hand. Coker simply dared not risk that awful
limerick going to Prout!

'Will you tell me what you've done with it?' breathed
Coker, at last.

'No, I won't.'

'You little fat scoundrel——'

'That will do!' said Bunter.

'Wha-a-t?'

'I said that will do! Don't be cheeky, Coker! I'm not
taking any lip from you, I can tell you,' said Bunter. 'Just
shut up.'

Coker almost exploded, at that. Harry Wharton and
Co. moved a little nearer. They really feared that Billy
Bunter was going to be massacred on the spot.

But Coker, with a Herculean effort, controlled his wrath.
That wretched limerick was hanging over his head like the
sword of Damocles—or Sophocles, as Coker preferred it.

The mere thought of Prout looking at it, and recognizing his hand-writing, made Coker feel cold all over. He would have chuckled with glee, had Prout looked at a typed copy, untraceable to the author. But that limerick in his own 'fist', known at once to be his handiwork, meant nothing short of an interview with the Head, and the almost certain sentence of the 'sack' to follow. Coker did not always realize that a fellow couldn't do just as he liked at school— but even Coker realized that a fellow could not call a member of the Staff a pompous old duffer who talked rot, and get away with it. Awful results impended over Coker if Prout saw that limerick. He glared at Billy Bunter as if he could have bitten him. But he did not bite! He simmered like a volcano on the point of erupting, but he did not erupt.

'Look here, Bunter——!' Coker forced himself to speak calmly.

'Rats!' said Bunter.

'Let me have that limerick——'

'Shan't!'

'You little fat rotter!' gasped Coker. 'What are you going to do with it?'

'I'm going to keep you on tender hooks!' said Bunter, doubtless meaning tenterhooks. 'And serve you right! I was going to give it to you yesterday, and you smacked a fellow's head before he could speak. Well, now you can whistle for it, see? I may let you have it back some time. I may not. Just at present, you can whistle for it, and be blowed to you! That's all.'

With that, Billy Bunter revolved on his axis, and walked away. Coker stood as if rooted, staring after him. Harry Wharton and Co. followed him, and the captain of the Remove dropped a hand on a fat shoulder.

'Look here, Bunter——!' said Harry.

Bunter blinked at him.

'Better let Coker have that limerick,' said Harry.

'I'll watch it.'

'He will be frightfully anxious about it,' said Bob Cherry.

'Let him!'

'It's too thick, old fat man,' said Frank Nugent.

'The thickfulness is too terrific, my esteemed fat Bunter,' said Hurree Jamset Ram Singh, with a shake of his dusky head.

'Cough it up,' advised Johnny Bull.

'No jolly fear!' said Bunter. 'He smacked my head when I was going to give it to him. Think a fellow likes his head smacked? Well, now he can whistle for it, see?'

'Well, yes, but——!' said Harry, doubtfully.

'Coker's too jolly high and mighty,' said Bunter. 'It will do him good to take him down a peg or two. Smacking a fellow's head! I can jolly well tell you fellows that I'm going to keep him on tender hooks, just as long as I jolly well like, so yah!'

And with that, Billy Bunter rolled away, and the Famous Five gave it up. Evidently, the fat Owl's fat mind was made up: Coker, who undoubtedly was a little too liberal with his head-smacking, was going to be kept on tenterhooks: which, in Billy Bunter's opinion, served him jolly well right!

Billy Bunter rolled away, grinning: and the Famous Five, dismissing the matter from mind, resumed cricket as a topic. But Horace Coker did not find it so easy to dismiss it from mind. It was a weighty matter to Coker: a matter, indeed, of the most tremendous importance. He, Horace James Coker, in his own esteem a most important person, was actually at the mercy of such an inconsiderable microbe as a fat fag in the Lower Fourth Form! He stood staring at a fat figure that rolled in the distance, his hands clenched quite convulsively: longing to stride after Bunter, and smack his fat head right and left, but——! But that fat little tick had hidden his limerick somewhere, and at any minute he liked could fish it out and let Prout see it! Even Coker realized that his short way with fags was of no use to him now.

'By gum!' breathed Coker. 'By gum! I'll smash him— I'll spiflicate him—if—if only he hadn't got that limerick! I—I—I'll——!' Coker glared at that fat figure, and brandished a fist in the air. Coker would have given a term's pocket-money, to land that fist on William George Bunter. But that limerick stood like a lion in the path, as it were. He had to be content with brandishing it at a grinning Owl.

'Coker!'

A deep voice boomed behind him.

Coker ceased shaking his fist, suddenly, and spun round at the voice of his form-master. Mr. Prout gave him a petrifying look.

'What are you doing, Coker?' boomed Prout.

'Oh! N-n-nothing, sir——' stuttered Coker.

'Why were you waving your hand in the air in that ridiculous manner, Coker?'

'I—I—I——'

'What does this mean, Coker? If seems that whenever I see you, you are performing some ridiculous antic. Have you taken leave of your senses, Coker?'

'Oh! No, sir! I—I——'

'Yesterday,' said Mr. Prout, 'I found you appearing in public in a dusty, dishevelled, disreputable state. Later I came upon you walking about bent double in a most extraordinary manner. Now I find you waving your arm in the air as if you were shaking your fist at some person. Is it

your object, Coker, to make yourself a figure of derision?
Have you no sense whatever of the dignity expected of a
senior boy in the Fifth Form? I will not allow a boy in my
Form to indulge in these absurd antics, Coker. Take a
hundred lines, Coker.'

Mr. Prout walked on, frowning. He left Horace Coker
in a frame of mind to which no words in the dictionary could
possibly have done justice.

CHAPTER 16

NO LUCK!

CRASH!

Peter Todd jumped.

There had been games-practice after class, and Peter was coming up to his study, No. 7 in the Remove, with a bat under his arm, when that sudden crash from No. 7 startled him. Peter shared that study with Tom Dutton and Billy Bunter. But he had left Dutton at the nets, and he had seen Bunter in the quad, so obviously neither of his study-mates was responsible for that crash. Someone else, it seemed, was in that study, where no one else had any business to be: and it sounded as if that unknown person was doing damage there.

'What the dickens——!' ejaculated Peter.

He ran on, to the study, and threw open the door, and stared in. What he saw there made him jump again. His eyes popped at Coker of the Fifth.

What a Fifth-form man could want in a junior study was a mystery. But Coker's actions were still more surprising than his unexpected presence. He had pulled out the table drawer. It was like Coker to give it such a hefty jerk that it came right out, landing its contents crashing on the study floor. Many things were kept in that table-drawer—odds and ends of cutlery, a bottle of gum, pens, pencils, compasses, and various other oddments—and all of them were now scattered over the floor, and Coker was staring down at them with a frowning brow.

'Not there!' grunted Coker, as Peter stared in. He did

not trouble to replace the drawer. He pitched it down on the articles it had contained. Peter, for a moment or two, stared at him quite blankly. Then he found his voice.

'What the thump do you think you are up to, in my study?' shouted Peter.

Coker was stepping towards the book-shelf. He stopped, and turned, and gave the Removite a glare.

'Keep out!' he snapped.

'Keep out of my own study!' gasped Peter Todd.

'Yes! Shut that door.'

Coker turned to the book-shelf again. There were a good many books on it, belonging variously to Peter Todd, Tom Dutton, and Billy Bunter. Coker's heavy hand grabbed at them. One after another he grabbed them, opened and shook them, and pitched them on the study table.

'Let those books alone!' roared Peter.

Coker did not even turn his head. He had neither time nor inclination to heed Peter. Coker was in search of something he was very anxious to find. Bunter had hidden his limerick somewhere: and he could hardly have hidden it elsewhere than in his own study. Coker had thought that out: and having thought it out, he had come up to No. 7 to search. He had been searching for some time, with no luck so far, when Peter Todd came up. Peter, who had never even heard of Coker's limerick, was astonished—but more exasperated than astonished. His study was rapidly assuming the aspect of a wreck. A Fifth-form senior ragging in a junior study was an unusual and unexpected phenomenon: but there was Coker, chucking things about right and left: and as he did not heed Peter's voice, Peter proceeded from words to actions.

A sudden jab, from a cricket bat, in the middle of his back, interrupted Coker's activities at the book-shelf.

'Oh!' gasped Coker.

He turned then. He had not heeded Peter's words, but he had to heed his bat. It was quite a painful jab.

'Now get out!' roared Peter. 'Think you can come here ragging in my study, you Fifth-form fathead? Jolly well get out, see?'

Coker rushed. Another jab from the bat, this time impinging upon his waistcoat, made Coker gasp, but it did not stop him. His mighty grasp closed on Peter.

'Now, you cheeky little smudge!' hissed Coker. The next moment, Peter was whirling through the doorway.

He landed in the passage with a bump and a roar. Coker slammed the door on him, and resumed his search. Probably Coker supposed that his short way with fags had disposed of Peter Todd. He resumed shaking out the books. That limerick was hidden in the study somewhere, and what more likely than that the fat Owl had hidden it in a book? Coker was going to ascertain, anyway.

But Peter Todd was very far from disposed of. Had it been Bunter who had come up to the study, no doubt Coker's methods would have been effective. But Peter was made of sterner stuff.

For some moments, he sprawled in the passage, gasping for breath. Then he scrambled up, red with wrath. Fellows, in the passage, stared at him. Vernon-Smith and Redwing, Tom Brown and Squiff, had come up, after the cricket. Skinner and Snoop were looking out of their study doorway further up the passage. Lord Mauleverer was coming along from No. 12, and Fisher T. Fish from No. 14. All of them stared at Peter.

'What's that game, Toddy?' called out the Bounder.

Peter spluttered breathlessly.

'Fifth-form man in my study, ragging,' he gasped.

'That mad ass Coker—lend me a hand, you men! Ragging things right and left—chucking things all over the shop— that potty fathead Coker——'

'Coker!' exclaimed Redwing. 'That fathead who came to the dorm last night——'

'Yes, that mad ass Coker of the Fifth——'

'Ragging in a Remove study!' exclaimed Smithy. 'By gum! We'll jolly soon give him something to cure all that.'

'What-ho—come on,' said Squiff.

There was a rush to No. 7. Skinner and Snoop remained onlookers, from their study, having no taste for a shindy with so hefty a senior as Horace Coker. But every other fellow in the passage joined in the rush.

The door of No. 7 was hurled open.

Coker had cleared the book-shelf, without finding what he sought. The books were scattered, some on the table, some on the floor, some on the armchair. Coker had no time to waste replacing them on the shelf. Now he was staring round the study, in search of some other possible hiding-place of that limerick. He gave the crowd of juniors in the doorway an angry glare.

'Keep out of this, you!' he snapped.

'Bag him!' shouted Smithy.

'Collar him!' gasped Peter Todd.

In a moment the study was swarming with excited juniors. One or two of them, perhaps three, Coker could have handled. But six or seven were too many and too much even for the hefty Horace.

He almost disappeared under the mob that swarmed over him. He went down with a bump, struggling frantically but in vain. Hands that seemed innumerable clutched and pinned him on all sides.

'Frog's march!' shouted the Bounder.

'Good egg!'

'Go it!'

They heaved Coker up from the floor. Struggling wildly, spluttering wrath, they marched him out of the study. Struggles did not help him. Peter Todd and Smithy had a leg each—Squiff and Tom Brown had an arm each—Redwing had a grip on a collar, and Lord Mauleverer lent a hand with a grasp on Coker's tousled hair. Hefty man as he was, Coker could do nothing but wriggle and splutter, as he was borne out of No. 7 Study.

A fat junior coming up the passage stopped to stare, in astonishment, through a pair of big spectacles.

'Oh, crikey!' ejaculated Billy Bunter. 'What's up? He, he, he! I say, you fellows, what are you ragging Coker for?'

'Caught him ragging in our study,' gasped Peter. 'Lend a hand, fatty. Take hold of his ears.'

Billy Bunter jumped.

'In our study!' he exclamed. 'Oh, crikey!'

Bunter did not stay to lend a hand. He shot past the crowd in the passage and shot into No. 7 Study. The fat Owl could guess why Coker had been in that study, if the other fellows couldn't. While Coker of the Fifth, in the midst of a hilarious crowd of Removites, went down the passage in the frog's march, Billy Bunter rushed across the study to the armchair, and lifted the cushion from the seat thereof. Under that cushion reposed a crumpled sheet of impot paper, adorned by Coker's well-known scrawl. It was the limerick!

Billy Bunter clutched it up.

Coker had not discovered it in its hide-out. But there was little doubt that he would have done so, given time. Evidently, it was not safe in Bunter's study: Coker might try again, and might not be interrupted next time. That limerick was transferred once more to a sticky pocket. Bunter had to find a safer hide-out for it, if he was going to keep Horace Coker on what he called 'tender hooks'.

At the moment, however, Coker was not bothering about that limerick. The Remove crowd, having frog's-marched him down the passage, and across the landing, dumped him down in the Fifth-form passage, where they left him for dead, as it were. For quite a long time after that, Coker was in no state to think about limericks, or anything else but gurgling for breath.

CHAPTER 17

IN SAFE KEEPING

TAP!

Click! click! click!

Tap!

Mr. Quelch heard the second tap. His fingers ceased to click the keys of his typewriter, and he glanced at the door.

'Come in!' rapped Mr. Quelch.

After class, that day, the Remove master was improving the shining hour, in his study, concentrating on his celebrated 'History of Greyfriars'. Sheaves of notes lay on his table, from which Quelch was typing out Chapter XXVIII— on the machine that Horace Coker had designed to borrow for his limerick. Deep in that congenial task, Quelch did not want to be interrupted: and there was a slight edge on his voice as he rapped out 'Come in'.

The door opened, and the fattest member of Quelch's form rolled into the study. Quelch eyed him inquiringly. He did not know why Billy Bunter had come there, nor did he know why the fat junior carried an envelope in a fat hand.

'Well?' rapped Mr. Quelch.

'If you please, sir——'

'Be brief!'

'Oh! Yes, sir! If—if you'd be so kind, sir, would—would you mind minding this for me, sir?'

Billy Bunter held up the envelope. Quelch gazed at it. The envelope was sealed. There was no superscription on it. It was a blank envelope: but evidently contained a paper of some sort. What it was, and why Bunter wanted him to mind it, Quelch had not the remotest idea. It was a very unusual request.

'What is it, Bunter?' asked Mr. Quelch.

'If—if you please, sir, it's a—a—a paper that I want to keep safe, sir, just a—a—a paper! I—I'm afraid I might lose it, sir. I—I lose things sometimes, sir, and—and it was nearly lost when a fellow came larking in my study after class. If you'd let me leave it here, sir, I should know that it was quite safe.'

Bunter laid the envelope on the table.

Mr. Quelch stared at it, and at Bunter. He was surprised, and a little mystified. Still, if a boy of his form wanted him to mind a paper to which he attached some value, the Remove master was quite willing to do so. Bunter, undoubtedly, was a fellow to lose things.

'That is a very odd request, Bunter,' said Mr. Quelch.

'Oh! Yes, sir! But if you wouldn't mind, sir——'

'Very well, Bunter: you may leave that envelope with me,' said Mr. Quelch. 'It will certainly be safe in my keeping.'

He picked up the envelope, and slipped it into a pocket.

'Oh! Thank you, sir,' said Bunter.

'Not at all, my boy,' said Mr. Quelch, benevolently.

He turned back to his typewriter. Billy Bunter backed out of the study, and did not grin till he had closed the door.

Click! click! click!

The machine was going again: and Quelch, deep in the History of Greyfriars School, forgot, in a few moments, that trifling incident: not only the envelope he had slipped into his pocket, but even the existence of that fat member of his form.

Billy Bunter rolled away, with a cheery grin on his fat face.

BUNTER LAID THE ENVELOPE ON THE TABLE.

By the window at the end of the corridor, a burly figure was standing. Billy Bunter blinked at it, and his grin widened. He was quite aware that Coker of the Fifth was on his track, and that Coker had trailed him to Masters' Studies. He had no doubt that Coker would be waiting for him to come out. And there was Coker—waiting!

But the fat Owl was not in the least alarmed. Coker made a stride towards him, perhaps expecting him to turn, and bolt up the corridor. But the fat Owl did not turn, and he did not bolt. He rolled on towards Coker of the Fifth, grinning: and did not seem alarmed, even when a heavy hand dropped on his fat shoulder.

'Got you!' breathed Coker.

Bunter gave him a blink.

'Want anything!' he inquired.

'I want that limerick, you fat little tick.'

'You can want!' said Bunter, cheerfully.

'Where have you put it?'

'In an envelope.'

'Well, where's the envelope, then, you young idiot!'

'Like to know?' grinned Bunter.

'I'm going to know—and I'm going to know now!' said Coker grimly. 'I'm not going rooting in your study again, you little fat tick, and getting mixed up with a mob of cheeky fags. I'm going to walk you off to wherever you've hidden that limerick, and get hold of it—and I'm going to smack your head, and keep on smacking it, until you tell me just where it is. Got that?'

'Okay,' grinned Bunter.

Coker gave him a glare. Bunter seemed to be amused: and his amusement was quite a puzzle to Coker. Bunter was in his grasp: there was no escape for him. His fat head was at the mercy of as many smacks as Coker chose to deliver.   Coker, having decided on these drastic measures, could see nothing to prevent him from carrying them out. Yet the fat Owl was not in the least alarmed.   He grinned.

'Well, where is it?' breathed Coker.   'You're going to tell me, and you're going to tell me now, see?'

'I don't mind telling you,' grinned Bunter.   'It's in Quelch's study.'

'Eh?'

'In Quelch's study.   You can go there and ask him for it, if you like,' said Bunter, cheerfully.   'I've sealed it up in an envelope, and asked Quelch to mind the envelope for me. He's got it now, in an inside pocket.'

Coker gasped.

'Quelch has got it?   Your beak?'

'Go and ask him for it!' grinned Bunter.   'Of course, if you said it was yours, Quelch would have to look at it, to see whether it was.   Would you mind?'

Coker gazed at him.   His heavy grasp fell from the fat shoulder.   He had been going to make Bunter, by main force, lead him to the whereabouts of that limerick.   But he did not want Bunter to lead him to a master's study for it!

'You—you—you——!' breathed Coker.

'He, he, he!' chuckled Bunter.   'Like Quelch to see it?'

Coker did not answer that.   But it was clear that he did not want Quelch to see it.   There was no doubt that any beak at Greyfriars, seeing a limerick referring so disrespectfully to another master, would immediately hand it to the master concerned.   It would be as fatal for Quelch to see it, as for Prout to see it.   If Quelch saw it, it would only be a matter of time, probably of minutes, before Prout saw it. And then——!   Coker could almost feel the 'chopper' coming down.

H

Coker's heavy hand rose. Only one solace remained to him—that of smacking Billy Bunter's fat head.

But even that solace was denied him.

'Better keep your paws to yourself, Coker,' said Bunter. 'You touch me, and I'll ask Quelch for the envelope, and I'll jolly well stick your limerick up on the notice-board for everybody to read! Like the idea?'

Coker's heavy hand fell again—not on a fat head!

The look he gave Bunter was devastating. If looks could have slain, the fat career of William George Bunter, of the Remove, might have come to a sudden termination on the spot. Fortunately for Bunter, looks couldn't. Having bestowed that basilisk-like glare on a grinning fat face, Coker turned away, and left him.

'He, he, he!' chuckled Bunter.

He rolled out into the quad, still chuckling. Coker was still on tenterhooks: and Coker was going to stay on tenterhooks, with that limerick in Quelch's safe keeping. Quelch, as he clicked happily on his typewriter, little dreamed of the use to which he was being put by a wily fat Owl.

CHAPTER 18

A STUDY SUPPER

'PREP!' said Potter.

Snort, from Coker.

'Prep, you know,' said Greene.

'Blow prep!'

'Prout may put you on con in the morning——'

'Blow Prout!'

Potter and Greene were at the study table, with their books. Coker might say 'Blow prep' and 'Blow Prout', but in point of fact, neither prep nor Prout could be 'blown' with impunity.

But Coker was in no mood for prep. He was striding about the study, while the other two sat at the table. Potter and Greene were getting on with the Carthaginian War, in Livy. Horace Coker was wholly, completely and utterly uninterested in the Carthaginian War. Coker had much more urgent matters to think of than ancient wars waged in Africa. Coker simply couldn't give any attention, just then, to any war in Africa, even to that great and historic war 'quod Hannibale duce Carthaginienses cum populo Romano gessere'. That war, at the moment, was to Coker a trifle light as air.

He came to a halt in his gloomy perambulation of the study, and stood staring at Potter and Greene with a corrugated brow.

'I'm in a jam,' he said. 'That rotten limerick may land me in an awful row. What's a fellow to do?'

'I wouldn't write limericks about beaks, if I were you,' said Potter.

'Not a safe game, Coker, old man,' said Greene, shaking his head.

'Fat lot of good telling me that, now,' snorted Coker. 'Now that I've made it up, and written it down, and that fat villian Bunter's got hold of it, and is holding it over my head like the sword of Sophocles.   Talk sense.'

'You'll have to get it back, somehow,' said Potter.

'I can't, when he's put it in an envelope, and asked his beak to mind it for him.   The artful young scoundrel!   If he'd kept it on him, I'd have had it fast enough.   If he'd kept it in his study, I'd have turned the place upside down and inside out till I found it.   But I can't get it back from Quelch, can I?'

'Um!' said Potter.

'Um!' echoed Greene.

'I daren't let him see it,' went on Coker.   'Of course he would hand it to Prout at once.   I can't even boot that young villian as he deserves.   He says he will ask Quelch for it, and stick it up on the board, if I do.   Fancy Prout seeing it there, and a crowd of fellows reading it.'

'Oh, crumbs!' said Potter.   'He would have a fit.'

'I wouldn't care if he had a fit: but he would walk me off to the Head, with that dashed limerick in his hand: and what would the Old Man do?   It might be the sack.'

'Likely enough,' agreed Potter.

'Most likely,' concurred Greene.

'The fact is, you'd better be civil to Bunter,' said Potter. 'He's got you in a cleft stick.'

'Civil to him!' breathed Coker.   'Why, I'm just longing to get my hands on him, and smash him up into little pieces.   I'd go and look for him now, and boot him all over the House, only—only—only——' Coker shook his head.   Booting Bunter was a happy, attractive, enticing thought. But it was not an idea that could be put into practice, in the circumstances. 'Look here, you men, what's a fellow to do?'

It was not like Coker to ask advice. A fellow who invariably knew best was not, naturally, much in need of advice. But his present predicament seemed to have brought Coker down a little from his lofty perch. Actually he condescended to ask Potter and Greene for advice.

Advice from Potter and Greene, however, proved no present help in time of need.

'You'd better do your prep,' suggested Potter. 'We've just on finished ours.'

'Yes: do your prep, old chap,' said Greene.

'You silly asses!' bawled Coker. 'Think I can bother my head about prep, with the sword of Sophocles hanging over my head? If you can't talk sense, shut up.'

Potter and Greene shut up, as bidden, resuming prep. Coker resumed perambulating the study, rather like a tiger in a cage.

Having, at length, finished prep, Potter and Greene rose from the table. Coker, coming to a halt again, eyed them almost inimically.

'Can't you fellows think of anything, except prep?' he demanded. 'I keep on telling you I'm in a jam. What's to be done?'

'What about a study supper?' asked Potter.

'What?'

'Lots left out of that parcel of yours, Coker.'

'Yes, what about it?' asked Greene. 'I'll trot it out of the cupboard if you like, Coker.'

Coker looked at them. His look was expressive.

'A study supper?' he said. 'Blow a study supper!

Here I'm in a jam, and you fellows talk about a study supper! Go and eat coke, the pair of you.'

He resumed perambulating.

Potter and Greene exchanged a glance, shrugged their shoulders, and put their books away. They bestowed a last glance on the study cupboard, in which reposed, as Potter had said, lots out of Coker's latest parcel from Aunt Judy. But Coker, evidently, was in no mood for study suppers: and they gave it up. As prep was over, and no supper in the offing, they went to the door, apparently not disposed to linger and watch Coker's gloomy perambulations.

Coker kicked the door shut after them, with a bang.

Then he perambulated once more.

'Oh, crumbs!' muttered Coker. 'What a jam to be in! All the fault of young Wharton and his gang—ragging a Fifth-form man in the quad! I've a jolly good mind to go along and thrash them all round.'

But he shook his head. Thrashing the Famous Five all round, even if a practicable proposition, would not have helped in the matter of the limerick. And that was where the shoe pinched.

The door opened, suddenly, without a tap.

Coker glared round. He was in no mood for callers. If Hilton, or Price, or Fitzgerald, or any other Fifth-form man, had dropped in, his reception would not have been hospitable. Indeed if Blundell, the captain of the Fifth, had looked in, to tell Coker that he was wanted in the Form eleven, Coker could hardly have been civil. But, as it happened, it was none of these. The caller who looked in at the door was not a Fifth-form man at all. He was a fat Removite.

Coker clenched his hands almost convulsively, as he
fixed a deadly glare on Billy Bunter.

Bunter eyed him warily through his big spectacles. He
had Coker, as Potter had put it, in a cleft stick. But he
knew the weight of Coker's hand, and he was wary.

'You!' breathed Coker. 'By gum, I'll——' He made a
stride towards the door. But he checked that stride.
'What do you want?'

'I've just looked in——'

'Get out!'

'Shan't!'

A couple of days earlier, a Lower-School fag who had
said 'Shan't!' to Horace Coker, would hardly have lived to
tell the tale. Now Billy Bunter said it quite coolly. And
Coker, instead of descending on him like a thunderbolt,
stood and looked at him. That limerick, reposing safely
in Quelch's pocket, which Bunter could pin up on the board
any time he liked, held Coker in thrall. Horace Coker had
heaps of pluck. He feared no foe. But he dared not lay
so much as a little finger on the fat junior in his doorway.
Bunter had only to ask Quelch for that envelope, and pin
that limerick up on the board for all Greyfriars to read, and
Coker's number was up.

'What do you want, you little fat rotter?' asked Coker,
in a choking voice.

'A little civility, to begin with,' said Bunter. 'Don't call
a fellow names, Coker! I don't like it! I don't expect
much from you in the way of manners, but there's a limit.
Bear that in mind.'

Coker could only gasp.

'You throw your weight about a good bit too much,'
went on Bunter. 'It won't wash with me, Coker, I can tell
you. I've no use for it. If you choose to be pally——!'

'Pally!' gurgled Coker.

'Yes, pally—if you choose to be pally, I'll stay for supper in this study. I'm not gone on the scramble in hall. What about it?'

'Think I'd have a grubby Remove fag to supper in my study?' bawled Coker.

'Please yourself,' retorted Bunter. 'I'm not the fellow to butt in where I'm not wanted, I hope. If you'd like me to stay, I'll stay, that's all. If not, I'll go. You've only to say the word.'

'Go!' hissed Coker.

'Oh, all right! I've got to see Quelch, as it happens, and I shall just catch him before he goes to Common-Room. I've got to ask for something he's minding for me. Something I'm going to stick up on the board. Cheerio.'

Bunter revolved in the doorway.

The desire to rush at him, and hurl him into the passage with a tremendous kick on his plump trousers, almost over-came Coker. But not quite! It would have been most enjoyable. But it certainly would not have kept Bunter from pinning that limerick up on the board.

'I—I—I say, hold on!' gasped Coker. There was no help for it.

Bunter blinked round at him.

'You—you—you——' Coker seemed hardly able to articulate. 'You—you—you can stay here to supper, if you like.'

'Oh, I don't know that I'm specially keen on it,' said Bunter, airily. 'I think on the whole I'll go down and see Quelch——'

'I—I say, do stop!' Coker could hardly get it out. But he got it out. 'I—I've got some jolly good things in the cupboard, Bunter—I had a parcel from my Aunt Judy yesterday.'

'Did you?' said Bunter. 'Well, if you'd really like me to stay to supper, Coker——'

'You cheeky little fat smudge——!' Coker broke out inadvertently.

'Oh! All right! I'll go.'

'I—I—I mean, stop! Stay to supper, Bunter. I—I— I'll be glad if you'll have supper in my study, Bunter,' gasped Coker.

'Well, if you put it like that, old chap, I'll stay,' said Bunter, and he rolled into the study.

He sat down at the table. And Coker, feeling like Vesuvius on the very verge of eruption, handed out Aunt Judy's good things from the cupboard: and Billy Bunter, feeling rather like a pig in clover, proceeded to deal with them.

CHAPTER 19

TARTS FOR BUNTER

'Looks sort of jolly, what?' said Bob Cherry.

'Sort of!' said Harry Wharton.

'The sortfulness is terrific,' grinned Hurree Jamset Ram Singh.

'Merry and bright, and all that!' remarked Johnny Bull.

'Quite a little ray of sunshine!' said Frank Nugent.

And all the Famous Five smiled. Those remarks were in a sarcastic vein. They were looking at Horace Coker, in the quad after third school the following day. Coker of the Fifth was looking anything but jolly, anything but merry and bright, and bore no resemblance whatever to a ray of sunshine.

Coker was leaning on one of the old elms, his hands driven deep into his trousers' pockets His brows were knitted. He did not waste a glance on the chums of the Remove. He seemed buried in deep and troublesome thoughts, like a fellow striving to solve a problem that had no solution. Generally exuberant, often a little too exuberant, Coker looked completely deflated. If all the troubles of the universe, and a few over, had landed in a heap on his burly shoulders, Coker couldn't have looked more pessimistic.

'What the dickens is up with him?' asked Bob. 'If he was going to be sacked, he couldn't look glummer.'

'Trouble with Prout, I expect,' said Harry. 'Coker's always in a row with his beak. Rough passage in form this morning, perhaps.'

'Hallo, hallo, hallo, what's Bunter up to?' exclaimed Bob, staring. 'By gum, the fat ass is asking for it.'

Billy Bunter rolled past the Famous Five, without bestowing a blink on them. He rolled up to Coker. And to their amazement, he addressed the Fifth-former in tones of easy familiarity.

'Oh! here you are, Coker, old boy.'

The Famous Five could only stare. Fifth-form seniors were not, as a rule, addressed as 'old boy' by juniors in the Lower School. Even a good-tempered Fifth-form man like Blundell or Fitzgerald, would probably have smacked the head of any fag who had walked up to him, in open quad, in the sight of all Greyfriars, and addressed him as 'old boy'. And Horace Coker was the most 'Fifth-formy' of all the Fifth. He was the very last senior in the school to take cheek from a Lower boy. In thus addressing Coker, Billy Bunter seemed not only to be 'asking for it'—he really seemed to be sitting up and begging for it.

Coker made quite a convulsive movement. His right hand came out of his trousers' pocket. Harry Wharton and Co. naturally expected to see it descend on William George Bunter, hard.

But it did not so descend. Slowly, reluctantly, it went back to Coker's trousers' pocket, leaving Bunter unsmitten.

'I've been looking for you ever since we came out, old chap!' went on Bunter, breezily.

Coker looked at him, without speaking. His look was expressive. But he made no move to slay Bunter.

'I say, old fellow, Mrs. Mimble's got in a fresh lot of cream tarts, at the tuck-shop,' said Bunter. 'Like some?'

Coker found his voice.

'No!' he uttered.

'Oh, come on,' said Bunter. 'I can tell you they're prime. Are you coming along, Coker?'

'No!' breathed Coker.

'Well, look here, Coker, if you don't want any I do,' said Bunter. 'I want a snack before dinner, if you don't! Come on.'

Again Coker made a sort of convulsive movement. But he did not stir from his tree, either to come on, or to slay Billy Bunter.

'Are we dreaming this, you men?' Bob Cherry questioned his comrades.

'Must be, I think,' said Harry Wharton, blankly. 'What the dickens is the matter with Coker?'

'The fact is, I've been disappointed about a postal-order, Coker,' went on Bunter. 'Otherwise, I'd stand treat. Look here, you shell out this time, and I'll shell out next. What? That's fair. Come on.'

'Get out!' breathed Coker.

'Eh! Did you say get out?' Billy Bunter frowned. 'I think I've told you, Coker, that I don't want any Fifth-form swank from you. I'm willing to be pally, if you are. If not——'

'You little fat frowsy frog, get out!' hissed Coker.

'Oh, all right! I'll cut in and speak to Quelch—I've got to ask him for something——' Bunter turned away.

Then Coker, at last, stirred.

'Hold on, Bunter. I—I'll come to the tuck-shop, if you like,' he gasped. He detached himself from the tree.

Billy Bunter turned back.

'Look here, are you coming, or not?' he snapped. 'I've no time to waste on you, Coker. Yes or no?'

'Yes!' gasped Coker.

'Come on, then, and not so much jaw,' said Bunter.

Really, the Famous Five could only wonder whether they were dreaming, as Billy Bunter rolled away in the

direction of the tuck-shop, and Horace Coker walked with
him. He went reluctantly. But he went.

'Anybody know what that means?' asked Bob Cherry.
'Coker taking orders from Bunter—and he's going to stand
him tarts at the tuck-shop! Has he gone crackers, or
what?'

'The crackerfulness must be terrific,' said Hurree Jamset
Ram Singh.

'Can't make it out,' said Nugent.

'He was asking for it!' said Johnny Bull. 'Asking for it
as hard as he could. And Coker took it like a lamb!
Coker!'

Harry Wharton knitted his brows. He remembered
a little scene from the day before, which the other fellows
had forgotten. He remembered the fat Owl's plan to keep
Coker on what he called 'tender hooks'. Coker had had to
'take it': just as he was 'taking it' now. If Bunter still had
that limerick, it accounted for what the Co. had just
witnessed: and really, there was no other way of accounting
for it. Twenty-four hours ago, Billy Bunter had thought
only of 'tit for tat': of keeping Coker on tenterhooks as a
reprisal for his too liberal head-smacking. It looked as if
the fat and fatuous Owl had been doing some thinking since,
and had realized the power that was in his fat hands, and
determined to use it for his own advantage. The captain
of the Remove frowned.

'Look here, you chaps, this won't do,' he said. 'I've
heard that Bunter had a study supper with Coker last
evening. Now he's making him stand tuck at the tuck-shop.
Has he still got that limerick?'

'That limerick!' repeated Bob.

'He had it yesterday—you remember how he talked to

Coker then? He was going to keep Coker on tenterhooks——'

'Tender hooks—I remember!' chuckled Bob.

'Serve him right for throwing his weight about so much,'
remarked Johnny Bull. 'He can't expect to smack fellows'
heads and get nothing back.'

'Well, yes, perhaps,' said Harry. 'But this is outside
the limit, if that fat ass is sticking him for tuck, and holding
that silly limerick over his head—and it looks like it.'

Bob Cherry whistled.

'Even Bunter wouldn't——!' he said.

'Well, it looks like it. Bunter's too fatheaded to understand that he's acting like a rascal: all he thinks of is tuck,
and paying Coker out for smacking his head. But if that's
how it is, it won't do.'

'It jolly well won't!' agreed Bob.

'We'd better look into it, I think, and if he's still got that
limerick, we'll make him cough it up, and hand it back to
Coker.'

'Yes, rather,' said Nugent.

'The ratherfulness is terrific,' agreed the nabob of
Bhanipur.

All the Famous Five were agreed on that. Billy Bunter's
fat intellect moved in mysterious ways its wonders to
perform: and very probably he did not realize the unscrupulousness of what he was doing. On that point the Co.
were prepared to educate him!

'Come on, then,' said Harry.

They walked to the tuck-shop, into which Billy Bunter
had disappeared with Coker. And when the fat Owl of
the Remove emerged from that establishment, with a fat,
shiny and sticky face, he found the Famous Five waiting
for him.

CHAPTER 20

BUMPS FOR BUNTER

'THIS way, Bunter!' said Bob Cherry.

He linked his arm in a fat one. Johnny Bull linked Bunter's other fat arm. Billy ·Bunter blinked at them alternately.

'What's on?' he asked.

'We are—to your little game,' answered Bob. 'Come along, old fat man. We want to talk to you.'

'Look here, you leggo!' squeaked Bunter. Two fat arms wriggled. Billy Bunter did not know what was 'on': but the expressions on five faces made him uneasy. 'I say, you fellows, leggo—I'm going to sit down on that bench——'

'Not at all! You're coming for a walk.'

'Shan't!' hooted Bunter.

Bob Cherry chuckled.

'You can say "Shan't" to Coker, so long as you've got his limerick,' he said. 'But it won't wash with us. We haven't been making up any limericks about beaks and leaving them spotted about the quad. Come on, you bad lad.'

Bob Cherry and Johnny Bull walked away, each in possession of a fat arm. Billy Bunter, like Eugene Aram, walked between. There was really no choice for the fat Owl. Harry Wharton, Frank Nugent, and Hurree Jamset Ram Singh, walked behind. Under that irresistible escort, Billy Bunter went, reluctantly. His reluctance increased, as the Famous Five walked him into the old Cloisters. He

121

'YOU'RE COMING FOR A WALK.'

realized that he was being marched out of the public view. He lagged, and dragged at his fat arms.

'Get on,' said Harry, from the rear.

'Shan't—yaroooh! Leave off kicking me, you beast!' roared Bunter. 'I—I—I'll come if you like.'

And he came.

In the Cloisters, his fat arms were released, but the Famous Five surrounded him in a circle. Billy Bunter blinked from one face to another, with growing uneasiness.

'Now, you fat villain——!' began the captain of the Remove.

'Oh, really, Wharton——'

'What have you done with Coker's limerick?'

'Eh!' Bunter blinked at him in astonishment. He had wondered uneasily what the chums of the Remove were 'up' to: without the remotest idea that it had anything to do with Coker or his limerick. 'Wharrer you mean?'

'You've still got it?' asked Harry.

'Perhaps I have, and perhaps I haven't,' retorted Bunter. 'Nothing to do with you fellows, is it?'

'Lots!' said Bob.

'The lotfulness is terrific, my esteemed and execrable Bunter.'

'You told us yesterday that you were going to keep it, and keep Coker on tenterhooks,' said Harry.

'So I jolly well am,' said Bunter. 'Think I'm going to have my head smacked for nothing? I'm jolly well going to keep him on tender hooks just as long as I jolly well like. I'll show him.'

'If that's all, I don't know that we'd butt in,' said Harry. 'But it looks as if that isn't all, Bunter. You had supper in Coker's study last night. Why did he let you?'

'Oh, we're rather pals, you know——'

I

'And now you've been sticking him for tarts at the tuck-shop. How come?' demanded Bob Cherry.

'I suppose a chap can stand a chap tarts if he likes.'

'Quite—only Coker doesn't like!' said Harry. 'Look here, have you been holding that limerick over Coker's head?'

'Of course I haven't,' yapped Bunter. 'How could I? Coker's a foot taller than I am. I couldn't hold anything over his head.'

'Oh, my hat!'

'Ha, ha, ha!'

'Blessed if I see anything to cackle at. You jolly well know that I couldn't hold anything over Coker's head.'

'Ha, ha, ha!'

'You fat chump!' roared Bob. 'That's a jolly old metaphor.'

'I don't care what it is. I couldn't hold anything over the head of a chap a foot taller than I am. Besides, why should I?'

'I mean, have you been using the silly limerick to scare Coker?' hooted the captain of the Remove. 'We all know that he might be sacked if Prout saw it. Is that why he is toeing the line? That's what I mean.'

'Well, why can't you say what you mean?' yapped Bunter. 'Making out that I could hold things over the head of a great big beast like Coker——'

'Is that how it is?' roared Bob. 'Is Coker standing you study suppers, and tarts at the tuck-shop, because you've got that limerick, and he's afraid that Prout might see it?'

'It's plain enough,' said Johnny Bull. 'Coker would rather spiflicate the fat tick than stand him tarts. Bunter's holding that limerick over his head.'

'Metaphorically!' grinned Bob.

'Is that it, Bunter?' demanded Nugent.

Oh! No! Nothing of the kind,' said Bunter, promptly. 'The fact is, we're rather pals——'

'Yes, Coker looked pally!' said Bob.

'He can stand me a study supper if he likes, I suppose,' said Bunter. 'Nothing to do with you fellows. I may have told him I might stick that limerick up on the board, or I may not. He may be scared about it, or he may not. He jolly well won't smack my head again in a hurry, anyway. He, he, he. Wouldn't he jolly well like to! But he jolly well won't! He, he, he!'

'This won't do, Bunter,' said Harry.

'Won't it?' said Bunter, defiantly. 'I can jolly well tell you that it jolly well will. Coker smacked my head. I'd jolly well smack his, now, as soon as look at him. Who's Coker?'

'You're not going to stick Coker for tuck, because you've got that limerick up your sleeve,' roared Bob.

'I haven't got it up my sleeve. I might drop it, if I had——'

'Oh, my hat! Why did they send him to Greyfriars, instead of to a home for idiots!' gasped Bob. 'Look here, Bunter, you've got to chuck this, and you've got to chuck it now. You're not going to stick Coker for one more tart, see?'

'I'm not a fellow to stick a fellow for anything, I hope, Bob Cherry. You fellows might—— You haven't got my principles. Not me! Still, one good turn deserves another. If Coker chooses to stand a fellow tarts when a fellow's been disappointed about a postal-order, why shouldn't he, when a fellow's doing him a good turn like I'm doing? Think he'd rather have that limerick pinned up on the notice-board! He, he, he!'

'So you've told him you'll pin it up on the board, if he doesn't stand you tuck!' exclaimed Bob. 'You fat villain——'

'You see, it's a quip prop quop!' explained Bunter.

'A whatter?' gasped Bob.

'A quip prop quop! That means one thing for another —something for something,' further elucidated Bunter. 'I'm surprised that you don't know what quip prop quop means, Cherry. Lot of good Quelch teaching you Latin.'

'Oh! A quid pro quo!' gurgled Bob. 'You mean you're getting a quid pro quo from Coker——'

'No, I don't! Think I'd take a quid, if he offered me one?' exclaimed Bunter, indignantly. 'If you think I'd stick a fellow for a quid because I've got that limerick, Bob Cherry——'

'Oh, help!' gasped Bob.

'Ha, ha, ha!'

'A quip prop quop is all right,' said Bunter. 'I wouldn't touch his quids with a barge-pole. But a quip prop quop is fair play. I keep his limerick dark, and he stands me a few spots of tuck till my postal-order comes. Of course it's only till my postal-order comes. I believe I told you fellows I was expecting a postal-order——'

'I believe you did, you fat fraud. So you think you're going on sticking Coker for tuck till your postal-order comes—that is, till he's an old, old man with a white beard——'

'Ha, ha, ha!'

'You're jolly well not!' added Bob, emphatically. 'One good turn deserves another, just as you said, you fat tick, and Coker did me a good turn on Monday—when a tramp was slogging me in the wood. I'm going to do him a good turn back. Where's that limerick?'

'Find out!' yapped Bunter.

'I'm going to hook it off you, and take it back to Coker. I suppose you don't know that you're acting like an unscrupulous young rotter, but you can take my word for it——'

'Beast!'

'Honesty is the cracked pitcher that goes longest to the well, and saves a stitch in time, my esteemed idiotic Bunter,' said the nabob of Bhanipur.

'If you're making out that I'm not honest, Inky——'

'Not much making out about it,' said Johnny Bull. 'Cough up that limerick, Bunter. It's going back where it belongs.'

'The fat owl has hidden it somewhere, from what we heard him telling Coker yesterday,' said Harry. 'Where is it, Bunter?'

Billy Bunter grinned.

''Tain't where you'll jolly well find it,' he answered.

'You're going to tell us,' said Bob. 'We're going to bump you till you do. That's why we've lugged you along to this nice quiet spot. Now, where's that limerick?'

'You jolly well mind your own business——'

'Bump him!'

'Here, leggo!' yelled Bunter, as hands grasped him. 'I'll tell you where it is if you want to know. You jolly well can't get after it.'

'Where is it, then?'

'In Quelch's pocket.'

'What!' exclaimed all the Famous Five together.

'So now you know!' sniffed Bunter. 'I've sealed it up in an envelope and asked Quelch to mind it for me. He doesn't know what's in the envelope—he, he, he! You fellows can go to him, if you like, and tell him, and get

Coker sacked! I should call it sneaking! I know you're not so particular as I am, but I don't think you ought to go sneaking——'

The Famous Five gazed at Bunter. Then, with one accord, they fell on him. If that limerick was parked in their form-master's pocket, obviously it was out of their reach. Luckily, Bunter was within their reach—not luckily for Bunter. Five pairs of hands swept the fat Owl off his feet.

Bump!

'Yaroooh!'

Bump!

'Whooooooop!'

Bump!

'Oh, crikey! Leggo! I say, you fellows, leggo. I say, I'll stand you a spread in Coker's study. I'll make him play up. A topping spread——'

Bump!

'Wow! ow! wow!'

The old Cloisters echoed to Bunter's roar.

'One more for luck!' said Bob Cherry.

Bump!

'Ooooooh!' roared Bunter.

Having thus impressed upon William George Bunter's fat mind what they thought of him, the Famous Five walked away, and left him rousing the echoes.

CHAPTER 21

SO NEAR YET SO FAR

'TE!' said Mr. Quelch, quietly but firmly.

'Me!' said Mr. Prout, with equal firmness.

Coker of the Fifth felt like snorting, as he heard them.

Coker never could have much patience with schoolmasters. They were, in Coker's valuable opinion, rather a silly lot. But this, Coker thought, was really the limit: two old donkeys walking in the quad, saying 'tay' and 'may'; whatever 'tay' and 'may' might mean, if 'tay' and 'may' meant anything, which Coker doubted.

That afternoon was a half-holiday at Greyfriars. A summer half-holiday was quite a happy occasion for most fellows. And in fact everyone at Greyfriars, with the solitary exception of Horace Coker, seemed to be enjoying life.

Harry Wharton and Co. were playing cricket, on Little Side, in a match with Temple, Dabney and Co. of the Fourth. On Big Side Wingate and his merry men of the First Eleven were at the same game. Both matches had a good many onlookers. Other fellows were happily occupied according to their varied tastes: Skinner and Snoop smoking surreptitious cigarettes in a box-room: Fisher T. Fish counting his money in his study: Hoskins of the Shell evoking strange discords from the piano in the music-room; Mark Linley swotting Greek: Wibley sporting over his property-box: Billy Bunter travelling slowly but surely through a large bag of cherries: everyone, in fact, improving the shining hour in one way or another—excepting Coker.

Coker, like Gallio of old, cared for none of these things. He tramped in the quad with a disgruntled brow.

His friends, Potter and Greene, were at the cricket. But Coker did not miss them: he had no use for Potter and Greene. They could not help him out of that 'jam': indeed they actually forgot that he was in a jam except when Coker reminded them.

That limerick weighed heavily on Coker's mind. He could hardly regret having written it: it was so witty, so brilliant, hitting Prout off to a T, and testifying what a brainy fellow Coker was. If only he had been able to carry out his astute plan, typing it on Quelch's typewriter, leaving a typed copy on Prout's study table, and another on the table in Common-Room! Prout would have raged, without a clue to the limericker.

But it hadn't worked out. That limerick had never been typed on Quelch's machine. The original document, in Coker's own unmistakable 'fist', was in an envelope in Quelch's pocket! And if it came to light——

Coker almost trembled at the thought.

And that fat little tick, that indescribable cheeky little fat blighter, Bunter of the Remove, could bring it to light, any minute he chose! Unless, somehow, Coker got it back from Quelch!

That was the idea working in Coker's mind now, as he gave his attention to the two masters walking and talking in the quad.

They walked up and down a path by the elms. Neither of them glanced at Coker leaning on a tree, with his hands in his pockets. They were not interested in Horace Coker. It was in quite another Horace that they were interested: Quintus Horatius Flaccus, to wit.

Quelch and Prout, in fact, were discussing an old bone

of contention between them.   Did Horace, when he wrote
the twenty-ninth line of the first ode in the first book,
begin it with 'te' or with 'me'?

Coker, as their remarks reached his ears, could hardly
suppress a snort.   That, Coker scornfully reflected, was the
kind of thing beaks would be talking about!

Horace might have written 'te' or 'me', or any other
pronoun in the whole Latin grammar, and Coker couldn't
have cared less.   But it was a matter of quite deep import
to Quelch and Prout.

Coker was watching Quelch. Bunter's envelope, he
knew, was in one of Quelch's pockets. Was there the
remotest chance of nobbling it? If it was in a pocket of
his gown, Quelch might leave his gown in his study some
time, and there might be an opportunity. Coker had to
recapture that limerick somehow. It was simply exas-
perating to know that it was within a few yards of him, yet
as utterly out of reach as if it had been sailing through the
outer spaces in a Sputnik—so near, yet so far!

'Consider, Prout!' Quelch was going on, quite unaware
that his remarks very nearly evoked a snort from a Fifth-
form man. 'Consider! The phrase "doctarum frontium"
could hardly apply to Horace himself—is it not obvious
that it must apply to Maecenas? Admitting this, it implies
"te" at the beginning of the line—certainly not "me".'

'But consider, Quelch,' came back Prout. 'The word
"me" occurs in all known manuscripts of the Odea—
never once "te".'

'True! But there is a gap of many centuries between
Horace's time, and the earliest of extant manuscripts.
Copy must have been made from copy, and copy from copy,
and an error has crept in. We all know printer's errors of

our own day—copyists would be even more liable to them than printers——'

'Such a theory, Quelch, would cast doubt on every line in the Odea, not only on the twenty-ninth of the first ode.'

'Not at all, Prout! We must be guided by reason. Consider—"Dis miscent superis" is obviously in contrast to "me gelidum nemus"—the former must refer to Maecenas, the latter to Horace—clear evidence, in my opinion, that it should be "te", and certainly not "me", in the twenty-ninth line.'

Mr. Prout shook a ponderous head.

Coker breathed very hard.

That sort of stuff, while he was all hot and bothered about his limerick! Nero fiddling while Rome burned was simply nothing to it!

'Let us go over the lines, Prout,' said Mr. Quelch. 'I have my Horace here.' He plunged a hand into an inside coat pocket.

Quelch was never without his pocket Horace.

His hand came out with a slim volume in it—a pocket edition of the Odes. Something else came out with the little volume. It was a sealed envelope, which fluttered to the ground unnoticed by Quelch.

It was not unnoticed by Coker! Coker's eyes popped at it! That was it—he was sure that that was it! It was a plain envelope, with no superscription. Coker guessed at once what it was—the envelope containing the limerick. Quelch, evidently, had slipped it into the same pocket as his Horace. Probably he had forgotten its existence. He did not even notice that he had inadvertently pulled it out with the book. That little book contained Horace's Odes: so Quelch was naturally blind to trifles. He opened the book.

Coker hardly breathed.

The fallen envelope had fluttered almost within Coker's reach. Dared he pick it up? Quelch, certainly, hadn't noticed it! Had Prout?

He could not venture to pick it up. But he did venture to extend a foot, and place that foot over it.

The envelope disappeared from view under the largest foot in the Fifth Form at Greyfriars.

Now, if only they walked on——

But Quelch had come to a halt, as he opened the book. Oblivious of Coker, he proceeded to read aloud:

'Te doctarum hederae praemia frontium
Dis miscent superis: me gelidum nemus——'

'One moment, Quelch,' said Mr. Prout. Prout was peering about him. 'I think you dropped something, Quelch.'

Coker could have hit him!

'Eh! what?' Quelch glanced round. 'What——?'

'A letter or something——'

'A letter!' Quelch groped in the pocket from which he had taken the book. 'Bless my soul! Thank you, Prout—it is not here—I must have dropped it. I should be very sorry to lose it—it belongs to a boy in my form who has asked me to mind it for him. But where is it?'

Both masters peered round—Quelch anxious, Prout puzzled. As Bunter's envelope was no longer in Quelch's pocket, it was plain that he must have dropped it: yet it was not to be seen. Both masters glanced at Coker, but naturally it did not occur to either that a Fifth-form fellow had planted a large foot on that envelope.

'Bless my soul! Where can it be?' exclaimed Mr. Quelch. 'Can you see an envelope lying about, Coker?'

Coker glanced down.

'I can't see any envelope, sir,' he answered. It was quite a veracious answer: Coker couldn't see it—through his own foot!

'It must be close at hand,' said Mr. Prout. 'I certainly saw it fall, when you took the book from your pocket, Quelch, though I did not notice where it fell—the wind can hardly have carried it far—Coker!'

'Yes, sir,' mumbled Coker.

'Kindly look for that letter, Coker,' said Mr. Prout, with asperity. 'I am surprised, Coker, that you are not already doing so. Look for that letter at once, Coker.'

Coker, breathing hard, looked to right and left, and round about, but without stirring from his spot. He could not stir from that spot without revealing the envelope under his foot.

Mr. Prout frowned portentiously.

'Coker!' he rapped.

'Oh! Yes, sir!' stammered Coker.

'Upon my word! Are you too idle, Coker, are you too lazy, are you too regardless of your form-master's wishes, Coker, to take a little trouble? You are not rooted to that spot, I presume, Coker?' Prout could be sarcastic.

'Oh! Yes—no—no, sir!' mumbled Coker.

'Look for that letter at once, Coker! It may have blown behind that tree. Look for it.'

There was no help for it: Coker had to shift. Slowly, reluctantly, he shifted: and a gimlet-eye immediately fell on the envelope hitherto concealed by an extensive foot. Mr. Quelch uttered an exclamation.

'Why, there it is! That stupid boy was standing on it.'

Quelch stooped, and picked up the envelope. It was immediately restored to his pocket.

'Upon my word!' boomed Prout. 'Coker! How dare

you? I repeat, Coker, how dare you? Coker, you were deliberately concealing that letter with your foot. What is the meaning of this, Coker? How dare you play such a trick—such an insensate trick, Coker? Are you in your senses, Coker? Your extraordinary antics of late make me doubt it! Coker, go to your study at once, and write me a Georgic! Not a word, Coker! Go!'

Prout raised a magisterial hand.

'Go!' he boomed.

Coker, with the deepest of deep feelings, went.

The two masters resumed walking and talking, thrashing out that vexed question of 'te' and 'me', with the concentration that so important a matter fully merited. They forgot Coker. And Coker almost forgot his limerick, as he sat in his study grinding out a seemingly interminable Georgic.

CHAPTER 22

THE BAD LAD

'I SAY, you fellows.'

'Scat!'

Five fellows, ruddy and cheery after cricket, frowned at Billy Bunter. The fat Owl was not in the good books of the Famous Five.

Moreover, they were, like Prout and Quelch, dealing with a problem. Their problem had nothing to do with the classics. Not a single member of the Co. would have cared a boiled bean whether Quintus Horatius Flaccus had written 'te' or 'me' in any Ode in the four books of the same. Their problem was one that often came the way of schoolboys—a shortage of coin of the realm. They were rather late for tea: but there was still time to join the scramble in hall, if it came to that. Tea in the study, naturally, was preferred, if the funds ran to it. So the Famous Five were, at the moment, a committee of ways and means: and interruptions were not wanted.

Bunter, however, did not 'scat'.

'I say——!' he recommenced.

'Hook it!' said Johnny Bull, tersely.

'But I say, like to come to a spread?' asked Bunter.

'Eh?'

'What?'

They gave Bunter attention, at that. In the penurious circumstances, an invitation to a spread was really the one thing needful. But it was rather surprising, for Bunter. Billy Bunter was a determined and almost irresistible

136

butter-in at other fellows' spreads: but seldom or never was he the founder of the feast.

True, Bunter could be generous, on the rare occasions when he had more than enough for his fat and ravenous self. But those occasions were very rare. Now it looked as if one of those rare occasions had accrued.

'I mean it,' said Bunter, perhaps reading doubt in five faces. 'If you'd like to come to a jolly good spread——'

'The likefulness would be terrific, my esteemed fat Bunter,' said Hurree Jamset Ram Singh. 'But——'

'But where's the spread?' grunted Johnny Bull. Johnny, evidently, doubted.

'Has that postal-order come, Bunter?' grinned Bob Cherry. 'Or are you talking out of your hat, as usual?'

'Oh, really, Cherry! I'm asking you fellows to a jolly good spread,' said the fat Owl, warmly. 'You fellows have stood me a feed sometimes. Well, now I'm standing you one. I can tell you it's going to be good. There's a cake— a jolly good cake—and two kinds of jam—ham and eggs, and sosses—and tarts and meringues. You don't often get a spread like that in your studies, I can tell you. Well, like to come?'

'Sounds good,' said Frank Nugent.

'The goodfulness is terrific.'

'Well, come on,' said Bunter.

The Famous Five exchanged glances. Billy Bunter was not, at the moment, popular with the Co. They were down, with a very heavy down, on his peculiar dealings with Coker of the Fifth. They had signified the same by bumping him.

On the other hand, they were in the sad state known as 'stony', and a study spread was very much more attractive than the scramble in hall. And really they could not help feeling that this was rather decent of Bunter—after that bumping! Being for once, apparently the founder of a feast, he was asking them to join up, forgetful of bumps. It would have been ungracious to refuse.

'Okay,' said Bob.

'We'll come!' said Harry Wharton. 'Thanks, old fat man.'

'Oh, not at all,' said Bunter, airily. 'You've had me to a feed more than once—and now it's my turn, see? Come on. It will be ready by this time, and no need to keep Coker waiting——'

The Famous Five, about to follow Bunter, came to a sudden halt.

'Coker!' repeated Harry Wharton.

'Coker!' exclaimed Bob Cherry.

'Yes—come on,' said Bunter, briskly.

'Is Coker coming to the spread—is that what you mean?' asked Harry. 'Is Coker going to be there?'

'Well, of course, we can't leave Coker out, in his own study,' said Bunter. 'But that's all right—there will be lots.'

'In Coker's study!'

'Yes—do come on.'

'You fat villain!' roared Bob Cherry. 'Are you sticking Coker for a spread in his study and asking us to loot him along with you?'

'Oh, really, Cherry——'

'Is that it?' gasped Nugent.

That, undoubtedly, was 'it'. They had all guessed it, at the mention of Coker's name. Billy Bunter, after all, was not in unaccustomed funds: he was not standing a study spread in No. 7 in the Remove. That spread was scheduled to take place in Coker's study in the Fifth—it was Horace Coker who was going to be the founder of the feast!

'You—you—you——' breathed Harry Wharton. 'You fat, foozling, footling——'

'Oh, really, Wharton——'

'By gum!' said Bob Cherry. 'You fat brigand——'

'Well, that's civil, I must say, when a fellow's asking you to a jolly good spread!' exclaimed Billy Bunter, indignantly. 'You fellows make out that I butt in at a feed, and never stand one—well, now I'm asking you to a tip-top spread, and all you can do is to call a fellow names. Ungrateful, I call it. Talk about a serpent's child being more ungrateful than a sharp tooth——'

They gazed at Bunter. They knew exactly how pleased Horace Coker would be to see a crowd of Remove juniors at a spread in his study! If the fat Owl could not realize the unscrupulousness of 'sticking' Coker for tuck, while that lost limerick held him in thrall, the Famous Five were not likely to see eye to eye with him. They were not going to that spread!

'It's all right,' explained Bunter. 'I'm going to tea with Coker, and I can take some friends if I like! Coker won't say no—he, he, he!'

'You dithering fat ditherer——'

'You bloated brigand——'

'Look here, Bunter,' said Bob Cherry. 'We all know that you haven't sense enough to go in when it rains: but even a dithering nitwit ought to be able to work out the difference between right and wrong. You're doing a rotten thing in holding that limerick over Coker's head, and sticking him for tuck. You're a bad lad, Bunter. Take my tip, and chuck it.'

Sniff, from Bunter.

'Do, Bunter,' urged Harry Wharton.

'I'll watch it!' said Bunter.

K

'Let Coker have his limerick back,' said Nugent. 'You can't go on like this, you fat ass.'

'Can't I?' grinned Bunter. He seemed to think that he could!

'It's a rotten trick,' said Johnny Bull.

'Beast!'

'Can't you see that it's unscrupulous, Bunter?' asked Bob.

Billy Bunter gave him an indignant blink.

'Me unscrupulous!' he said, warmly. 'Well, I like that! If you fellows were as scrupulous as I am, you'd do. Not that you're ever likely to be! You haven't got my principles! Not high-minded, like me!'

'Oh, scissors!'

'Look here, are you coming or not?' demanded Bunter.

'Not!' answered five voices in chorus.

'Please yourselves,' snorted Bunter. 'You're turning down a jolly good thing, I can tell you. I told Coker I'd bring a few friends, and there's lots! You can't jolly well make out that I never stand a feed, when I'm asking you to a topping spread in a senior study, with lots and lots!'

'You fat fraud——!'

'Oh, all right! If all you can do is to call a fellow names, when he asks you to a spread, I jolly well won't take you now, so yah!'

And with that, the indignant Owl rolled away.

Bob Cherry made a motion with his foot—but checked it. Really Bunter, according to his lights, had been quite a generous Bunter, in asking the Famous Five to that spread. He was generously prepared to share 'lots and lots' with them—in Coker's study! He rolled away unkicked.

Evidently, Bunter did not realize that he was a 'bad lad'

at all. Perhaps he did not want to realize it: and Bunter
had an almost infinite capacity for believing just what he
wanted to believe! No doubt Bunter had a conscience:
but his fat conscience was not going to stand between him
and the ample supplies of tuck in Horace Coker's study.

'The fat ass!' said Bob.

'The fat rascal!' grunted Johnny Bull.

'Well, this won't do!' said Bob. 'If he won't cough up
that limerick—and he won't—we shall have to do something about it.   Coker did me a good turn, and it's up to us.
How can we get that limerick back for Coker?'

'Echo answers how!' said Nugent.

'Esteemed echo answers that the howfulness is terrific!'
sighed the nabob of Bhanipur.

'If we could——!' said Harry.

'We're going to—somehow!' declared Bob. 'Coker's a
howling ass, and a dithering fathead, and we've had lots of
rows with him, and I daresay we shall have lots more: but
we're not letting this go on.   Only—what can we do?'

'There's one thing we'd better do,' said Johnny Bull.

'What's that?'

'Cut into hall before the last doorsteps are gone.'

'Fathead!' said Bob. 'Still, perhaps we'd better.'

And they did.

Over those 'doorsteps' in hall, Bob Cherry's brows were
wrinkled.   Coker, obstreperous ass as he was, had done him
a good turn: and one good turn deserved another.   Bob
was going to see Coker through, if he could—but 'how' was
not so easy to decide.   A good turn to one member of the
Co. was a good turn to all: and Bob's chums were keen
enough to help—if there was anything to be done.   The
difficult question was, what?   Coker, through his own
unthinking fatheadedness, was in danger of the 'sack': and

Coker had rescued Bob from a severe hammering under knuckly fists. It was up to the Co.—if they could help! But for the present, at all events, the trump card was in the fat hands of that bad lad, Billy Bunter.

CHAPTER 23

BOOTS FOR BUNTER

'THERE he goes!' said Coker.

'Eh, what?' said Potter.

'Who?' said Greene.

'Quelch!'

Coker was standing at his study window, after class the following day. He was gazing out with a clouded brow.

He had quite a pleasant view from that window—the old quad, and the leafy elms: a crowd of fellows with cheerful faces: old Gosling sunning himself at the door of his lodge: Harry Wharton and Co., all looking merry and bright, going out at the gates. All these, however, did not attract a glance from Coker. His eyes fixed on a somewhat angular figure: that of Mr. Quelch, the master of the Remove. Quelch, in coat and hat, was apparently going out: but he had stopped to speak to Mr. Prout on his way: possibly on the perpetual and entrancing problem of 'te' and 'me'.

It was rather unusual for any fellow to be deeply interested in the movements of the master of another form. But Quelch was the object of Coker's deepest interest, these days. That fatal limerick was in Quelch's pocket: unknown to him, but only too dismally known to Coker. Often and often was Coker's eye on Quelch—perhaps in the hope that he might drop that envelope again. So far, Quelch hadn't. If Coker was waiting and watching for history to repeat itself, history had not obliged.

'Quelch!' repeated Potter, puzzled. 'What about Quelch?'

Potter and Greene had come up to the study in expecta-
tion of tea. Sad to relate, they had, for the time at least,
forgotten that limerick, and the sword of Damocles
impending over Coker's head.

But there were no signs of tea in the study. True, Aunt
Judy's parcel had been exhausted—chiefly by Billy Bunter.
Still, as Coker was rolling in money, that need have made
no difference. But it appeared that other matters were
occupying Coker's mind.

'He's going out,' said Coker.

'What about it?' asked Greene.

'I wonder——!' said Coker, meditatively.

'Well?' said Potter and Greene together.

'He's off on one of his grinds,' said Coker. 'You know
him—miles along the cliff road—he walks the other beaks
off their legs when they go with him. I wonder——!'
Coker paused again. 'It would be like him to take that
idiotic Horace out of his pocket and squint at it,
wouldn't it?'

'Quite,' said Potter. 'What about it?'

'He might drop that envelope again, if he did. I told
you about yesterday, when he dropped it and I got my foot
on it, only old Pompous spotted it, and I got a Georgic—
what are you grinning at, I'd like to know?'

Potter and Greene ceased to grin, at once, under an
almost ferocious glare from their harassed chum.

'Nothing to grin at!' hooted Coker. 'Have I got the
sword of Sophocles hanging over my head, or haven't I?
I wonder whether Quelch might drop it! It's in the same
pocket as his silly Horace, I know that.'

'Not likely,' said Potter, and Greene shook his head.
Really, it was not likely: Coker seemed to them rather like
a drowning man catching at straws.

'Well, I've got to get hold of it, somehow,' said Coker, moodily. 'I'm under that fat little beast's thumb till I do. Can't you fellows think of something? How can I get it back from Quelch?'

'You can't!' said Potter.

'Not unless you can get somebody to up-end him and pick his pocket!' said Greene, flippantly.

It was no time to be flippant! Fortunately, Coker did not perceive that this was flippancy. He looked quite thoughtful.

'Well, that's an idea, if I could get somebody to do it,' he said. 'But who? We couldn't do it ourselves——'

'Oh crikey!' gasped Potter and Greene simultaneously at the bare idea of performing such an exploit.

'It would be the sack for handling a beak,' said Coker. 'We simply couldn't do it, Greene. It's an idea—but it wouldn't work. Of course, I'm entitled to get hold of that limerick any way I can—it's mine. But it's no good suggesting collaring the old bean and yanking it out of his pocket.'

'I didn't mean——!' began Greene.

'Never mind what you meant—it wouldn't work,' said Coker. 'Try to think of something a bit more sensible.'

'Well, what about tea?' asked Greene. That seemed a sensible suggestion, to Greene.

'Never mind tea,' said Coker, irritably. 'I'm not thinking about tea—I'm thinking about that dashed limerick in Quelch's pocket. That young villain Bunter will very likely butt in for tea—he did yesterday!' Coker knitted a fierce brow. 'By gum! Won't I spiflicate him—if only I can get hold of that limerick! Won't I pulverize him! Hallo!' He glanced from the window again. 'Quelch has gone out! I fancy I'll follow on. After all, he might

drop that envelope again—he did once, right under my
nose, but for old Pompous I'd have had it.'

Coker crossed to the door.

'But I say——!' began Greene.

'I say——!' commenced Potter.

Coker did not stay to listen to what they had to say.
He tramped out of the study and down the passage.
Evidently Coker was clinging to the faint, faint hope that
history might repeat itself with that envelope in Quelch's
pocket.

Potter and Greene looked at one another, expressively.

'Ass!' remarked Potter.

'Chump!' said Greene.

'I'm getting fed up with his dashed limerick,' said Potter.
'What did he want to write the silly thing for, in the first
place? What did he want to strew it around the quad for?
Bother his limerick! I wonder if there's anything left
for tea?'

Potter opened the study cupboard. Generally there
were good supplies there at tea-time. Sometimes Potter
and Greene contributed: but the great provider was Horace
Coker. Potter and Greene would have scorned the idea of
sponging on old Horace: but their own resources were
limited, while Coker practically rolled in pound notes.
Coker was an open-handed fellow, who liked spending his
money freely: and undoubtedly his friends liked to see
him doing it.

But on this occasion, the cupboard in the study bore a
quite painful resemblance to that of Mrs. Hubbard. It was
bare! No doubt that was chiefly attributable to Billy
Bunter.

'Not much here, Greeney,' said Potter.

'Coker had lots yesterday,' said Greene.

'Yes, but he had that little fat rotter Bunter to tea. He has to jump when that fag says jump!' said Potter, sarcastically. 'I'd jolly well sling him out on his neck, and chance it.'

'Um!' said Greene, doubtfully. 'It's the sack for old Coker if that limerick comes out. Well, we may as well go down to hall, if there's nothing here.'

There was a step in the passage and a fat face looked into the study. Then a fat figure rolled in.

'Hallo, where's Coker?' asked Billy Bunter, blinking round the study through his big spectacles.

Potter and Greene eyed him inimically. Quite a large assortment of good things, which normally would have come their way, had been parked inside Billy Bunter's extensive circumference. Now, apparently, he had come for more—it looked as if he was going to make a habit of teaing in that study. Coker certainly, could not venture to say him nay. But Coker was not present now—and it occurred to Potter and Greene simultaneously that this was quite a good opportunity to let Bunter know what they thought of a grubby fag barging into the study.

'Coker's gone out, Bunter,' said Potter.

'Has he! After I told him I was coming up to tea!' exclaimed Bunter. 'I—I mean, after he asked me to tea. Well, I suppose I'd better wait for him.'

'I don't think you'll wait here for him,' said Potter, with a glance at Greene, who grinned.

'Eh! Why not?' asked Bunter.

'Because we're going to kick you out of the study!' explained Potter. 'Go it, Greeney.'

'What ho!' said Greene.

Billy Bunter gave them an alarmed blink. With Coker in the study, he was at his ease there: he had the hapless

Horace almost feeding from his hand! But there was no one now to stop Potter and Greene kicking him out of the study—and after that alarmed blink at them, Billy Bunter made a jump for the doorway.

Two kicks landed on him as he jumped—one from Potter, one from Greene. Billy Bunter roared as he received them.

'Yaroooh!'

The fat Owl bolted down the passage. After him rushed Potter and Greene, dribbling him as far as the landing. There Bunter dodged into the Remove passage, still yelling: and Potter and Greene, feeling a little better, went down to hall to tea.

CHAPTER 24

COKER KNOWS HOW

'Cor!' breathed Mug Parkiss.

His unwashed face registered alarm.

It was several days since Mug had seen that big, brawny schoolboy whose hefty fists had hammered him right and left. He did not want to see that out-size in schoolboys again, especially at close quarters. Now his shifty eyes fell on Horace Coker.

Mug was sitting, or rather sprawling, in the gully that led down from the cliff road to the beach. He sat at the foot of a chalk rock, against which he leaned a lazy back. Looking down the gully, he had a view of the ribbed seasands, and the blue sea rolling beyond, dotted with sails. But that view did not attract Mug. Mug was sucking at an empty pipe: and he was, at the moment, scraping through frowsy pockets in search of some remnant of tobacco, mingled with dust, to cram into the pipe. Also, it was a warm afternoon, and Mug was conscious of thirst. Mug would have given all the sea-views on the pleasant coast of Kent for the price of one pint of bitter at the Cross Keys.

Mug had that rocky gully all to himself. Only one person had passed while he sat there—a rather tall, angular gentleman, who gave him a glance of disfavour as he passed on, and went down to the beach. Mug's shifty eye had followed that angular gentleman malevolently. He would rather have liked to give Mr. Quelch a 'oner' in return for that disfavouring glance.

149

However, Mr. Quelch disappeared down the gully, and Mug resumed his search of frowsy pockets for frowsy remnants of shag. Then Coker happened along.

Coker came tramping down the gully: and Mug murmured, 'Cor!' and eyed him stealthily as he came. Mug had no objection to a spot of trouble, as a rule: but he had had more than enough of Coker's brawny fists. His alarm increased as that big schoolboy came to a halt, only a few yards from him.

But Coker did not, for the moment, notice the tramp sitting in the shade of the chalk rock. His eyes were on the figure in advance of him. He came to a halt as Mr. Quelch disappeared round the cliff at the foot of the gully.

Coker's face was gloomy.

With that faint, faint hope that history might repeat itself, he had trailed Quelch on his 'grind'. Quelch, quite unconscious that he was shadowed by a Fifth-form man, never dreaming that any Fifth-form man could be interested in an envelope in his pocket, had walked on and on, with his long vigorous strides: through Friardale village, along the cliff road, and now down the gully to the beach—never showing a sign of stopping for a rest. If he had, he might have taken out his pocket Horace: he might—imaginably—have shed that envelope, as he had done the day before in the quad—but he had done nothing of the kind. Even Coker realized that it was too much to hope for—and he doubted whether it was any use to keep on.

'Blow!' growled Coker.

In his study at Greyfriars, Coker had scornfully disregarded tea. But he had a healthy appetite: and he was conscious now that it was past a meal-time. He stood in doubt: whether to trail Quelch on the beach, with a faint lingering hope of a spot of luck: or to walk back to the school and provender. Then, as he stood, his eyes fell on Mug.

That chance encounter did not alarm Coker: he was quite ready, if required, to give the tramp some more of the same! But it alarmed Mug, whose unwashed features still bore traces of Coker's knuckles, and who most distinctly did not want any more of the same!

''Ere, you keep orf, you!' mumbled Mug.

'You, is it?' snapped Coker.

In his present mood, it would have been rather a relief to Coker to punch somebody. He would not have been displeased had Mr. Parkiss renewed hostilities. But as Mr. Parkiss showed no such intention—rather the reverse—Coker gave only a sniff, and turned away.

Then, suddenly, he turned back.

He fixed his eyes on Mug Parkiss. Back into his mind came what Greene had said in the study. It had not penetrated Coker's powerful brain that Greene's remark had been merely flippant. He had turned it over in his mind as a possible solution.

No Greyfriars fellow, of course, could think of collaring a 'beak' and dragging an envelope from his pocket. Such an exploit would mean an immediate interview with the Head, and the next train home. But suppose a fellow got some other person outside the school to do that very thing?

Coker's brain was working, as he stared at Mug.

Why not?

That limerick was his property—he was entitled to recapture his own property. That frowsy fellow looked as if he would do anything for a pound or so. No harm would be done. It would be a surprise to Quelch, if a tramp suddenly pounced on him, on the beach, up-ended him, and hooked an envelope out of his pocket. No doubt it would be quite a surprise! But Quelch wouldn't be hurt, and he would lose nothing, except that limerick that belonged to Horace Coker.

Why not? Coker breathed hard, as he thought it over, his eyes on the frowsy object sprawling against the chalk rock.

Mug watched him warily, in dread of hostilities. And as Coker, at last, made a step towards him, Mug scrambled up.

'You keep orf!' he gasped. 'I don't want no more trouble with you. You jest keep orf.'

'Don't go!' snapped Coker. Mug was edging away, preparatory to flight. 'Stop where you are, and listen to me.'

Mug eyed him.

'Wotcher want?' he inquired. He realized that it was not hostilities that he had to expect from Coker.

'I think you could do something for me,' said Coker. 'I suppose you'd like to earn a quid.'

Mug displayed no enthusiasm whatever. Certainly he would have liked a 'quid'. But he had a strong objection to earning one. Work had no appeal for Mug. Mug was not looking for a job.

'Did you see a gentleman pass here a few minutes ago?' went on Coker. 'A rather bony old bean.'

'I seed 'im!' grunted Mug. 'Looked at a bloke like dirt, he did. Wot about 'im?'

'I want something he's got about him,' said Coker.

Mug's eyes widened.

'He's a master at my school,' explained Coker. 'He's got a paper in an envelope in his pocket, that belongs to me.'

'Cor'!' said Mug, blankly.

'Mind, it belongs to me,' said Coker, sharply. 'It's a

paper I wrote, and a cheeky little beast got hold of it, and stuck it in an envelope, and asked that old bean to mind it for him. ' He doesn't know it's mine, but it is, see?'

'Cor'!' repeated Mug.

'Well, I want it,' said Coker. 'It's mine, and I want it. I can't do anything about it myself, as he's a beak at my school. Anybody else could. You could.'

'Oh!' said Mug. He began to understand.

'It's sealed up in a plain envelope, and he parks it in an inside pocket,' went on Coker. 'He's gone down to the beach now. If you could get that envelope off him, and bring it to me, I'd stand you a quid.'

'Blow me tight!' said Mug. 'I could 'andle him all right.'

'Mind, no rough stuff!' said Coker, warningly. 'If you hurt so much as a hair of his head, I'll hammer you black and blue. I just want you to get that envelope off him, any way you can: but take jolly good care that you don't damage him, or you've got it coming. You could tip him over, and grab that envelope—and cut! See? Easy enough, as he couldn't be expecting anything of the kind. It's worth a quid to you if you bring that envelope to me here.'

Mug eyed him very curiously.

'Just a plain envelope with some paper in it?' he asked.

'That's all,' said Coker.

'And its yorn?' grinned Mug.

'You frowsy rogue, do you think I should want it if it wasn't mine?' roared Coker, clenching a pair of large fists.

Mug Parkiss jumped back.

'All right, all right, it's yourn, if you say so!' he gasped. 'I'll do it for a quid, guvnor. Ready and willing. You wait 'ere and leave it to me. Jest a plain envelope in an inside pocket, says you! All right—I'll 'ave it off him in a jiffy! You jest wait for me 'ere, guvnor, while I get arter 'im.'

'Get going then,' grunted Coker.

Mug Parkiss got going. Coker watched him tramp down the gully, and turn the corner of the cliff below. He was feeling quite relieved, as he waited for Mug's return—with that envelope! It had seemed that there was no escape from his painful predicament, under the fat thumb of that bad lad Bunter. But Coker, after all, knew how!

CHAPTER 25

FIVE TO THE RESCUE

'WARE beaks!' breathed Bob Cherry.

'Oh! Bother!'

'The botherfulness is terrific.'

'Quelch!' said Johnny Bull.

'Dodge!' said Frank Nugent.

The Famous Five lost no time in 'dodging'. It was, in the circumstances, necessary to dodge. Time and place were not appropriate for an encounter with their form-master.

Not that there was any harm being done. The chums of the Remove were out of school bounds, that was all. They were sauntering, cheerfully and contentedly on the golden beach, heading for the gully that led up to the road over the cliffs, and to the village of Pegg. On half-holidays, Pegg and its environs were within school bounds. On other days, they were not. Had it been Wednesday, it would have been all right. On Thursday it was not all right. Extended bounds applied only on half-holidays—a little circumstance liable to be overlooked by unreflecting youth!

Harry Wharton and Co. when they went out for that ramble after class, had rather overlooked it. So, as they sauntered towards the gully, it was dismaying to behold a well-known angular figure descending therefrom—that of their form-master, Henry Samuel Quelch. At the same time, it was rather fortunate that they spotted Mr. Quelch before they reached the gully, as otherwise they, going up, would have met him face to face, as he came down.

As it was, there was time to 'dodge'.

Quelch was not looking in their direction: the gully was steep, and he was watching his step, as it were, as he came down. There was time to dodge, and there was ample cover at hand. The sands of Pegg were dotted with great chalk boulders. It was quite easy to slip out of sight, and remain unseen till the Remove master had gone on his way. The alternative was 'lines': and nobody wanted lines.

'This way!' breathed Bob.

He darted behind a great chalk boulder, near the towering cliff. His comrades were only seconds behind him. A moment ago, there had been five figures on the beach: now there were none. Even Quelch's gimlet-eye could only have discerned a stretch of sand as solitary as the beach of Robinson Crusoe's island. Not a soul was to be seen, as the Remove master emerged from the gully, and came along the sands.

Quelch was coming along with his usual vigorous strides, and in a few minutes his footsteps, grinding on pebbles, were audible to five pairs of ears behind the big boulder. He was coming quite near that boulder: but even eyes as keen as gimlets could not see through solid chalk, and the chums of the Remove had only to wait till he had passed.

They waited—silent.

Closer and closer came those footsteps, till they were quite close at hand. Then, suddenly, they stopped. There was silence.

'Oh, my hat!' breathed Bob.

The five juniors exchanged startled glances. They had naturally expected Quelch to walk on. He had not walked on: he had stopped. Did that mean that he had spotted something?

A long minute passed, anxiously. There was still no sound of footsteps. Harry Wharton ventured, at last, to

peer round the corner of the boulder. Then he had a
back view of Mr. Quelch.

Quelch had stopped, to sit down on a smaller boulder,
at a little distance towards the sea. He had taken a little
book from his pocket. Remove fellows knew that little
book by sight. It was Quelch's pocket Horace. Quelch
was already deep in the Odes!

'Oh, scissors!' murmured Harry.

'What——!' breathed Bob.

'He's squatted down to read his dashed Horace. Goodness only knows how long he's going to stop! What rotten
luck!'

'The rottenfulness is terrific.'

'Quiet—he might hear—he's only five or six yards away.'

'Blow!' mumbled Johnny Bull.

'We've got to wait——'

'We can't wait long—we shall be late for gates,' muttered
Nugent.

'Oh, blow!' said Bob.

All the juniors, in turn, peered out. There was Quelch
—a fixture! Form-masters did not have to bother about
'gates'. Quelch, absorbed in Quintus Horatius Flaccus, did
not have to count the minutes. To him, they probably
flew: while to the five juniors in cover, they seemed almost
endless.

'What about chancing it?' murmured Bob Cherry, at
last. 'If Quelch doesn't look round, we could whiffle along
the cliff, and cut up into the gully——'

'If!' said Johnny Bull.

Harry Wharton shook his head.

'Quelch always looks round at the wrong moment,' he
said. 'Better stick it out.'

More minutes passed. From behind their boulder, the

juniors, looking along the rugged face of the cliff, could see the gully at a distance. Quelch looked a fixture—his back to them. There was a chance, if he did not look round. But if he did——!

'Hallo, hallo, hallo!' murmured Bob. 'Here comes somebody!' A figure appeared in the gully, coming down to the beach. Bob stared at that figure—a frowsy, tattered figure that he remembered. 'My hat! That tramp!'

'Eh! Who?' asked Harry. The man coming out of the gully was a stranger to four members of the Co. Only Bob had seen him before.

'That tramp I told you about,' said Bob. 'The brute who pitched into me last Monday, when I tumbled over him in Friardale Wood, and old Coker came up and slogged him off.'

'Oh! That fellow,' said Harry: and all the juniors looked at Mug Parkiss, as he emerged from the gully, and came out on the sands. 'Keep close,' added the captain of the Remove. 'Don't let him spot us! One word from him would give us away to Quelch.'

Hugging cover, the juniors peered cautiously round the boulder at Mug Parkiss. His actions were a little peculiar. He stood for some moments staring round him on the beach, as if in search of someone. He did not glance towards the boulders piled near the cliff—it was the open sands that he was scanning. They saw him give a nod, and a grin overspread his unwashed stubbly face, as if he had seen what he was looking for. His shifty eyes fixed on the Greyfriars form-master, sitting on the chalk rock near the sea.

He moved on, and the juniors could see that he was treading softly and cautiously, making no sound on the sand. And the course he was following was leading him behind the seated form-master.

Bob Cherry caught his breath.

'See that?' he whispered. 'Is he after Quelch?'

'Looks like it,' said Harry.

It did undoubtedly look like it! Slowly, softly, cautiously, Mug Parkiss was approaching Mr. Quelch from behind. Every now and then he glanced quickly up and down the beach, as if to make sure that no one was about—happily unconscious of five schoolboys bunched behind the big boulder near the cliff. It certainly did look as if the tramp, taking advantage of the apparent solitude of the spot, had designs on Quelch.

Johnny Bull's jaw jutted.

'If that brute goes for Quelch, we're jolly well going for him, lines or no lines!' he said. 'If he's after Quelch's wallet, he's not getting away with it.'

'No fear!' said Nugent.

'The no-fearfulness is terrific!' murmured the nabob of Bhanipur.

'Quiet!' whispered Harry. 'If he lays a finger on Quelch, we'll handle him fast enough, if that's his game. But wait!'

They waited—watching, with growing excitement. Nearer and nearer Mug Parkiss drew to the unconscious school-master. Quelch heard nothing—and he did not look up or look round. The immortal verses of Quintus Horatius Flaccus absorbed him. He was absolutely at the mercy of the tramp—if Mug had hostile designs.

That was scarcely to be doubted now: but the juniors waited, and watched, to make sure. They did not want lines for rambling out of bounds: but lines or no lines, they were not going to remain idle if that ill-favoured ruffian handled their form-master.

Mug stopped at last, directly behind Quelch. Once

more he cast a glance up and down the shelving sands.
Then, suddenly, he pounced.

So suddenly, so swiftly, that even the watching juniors
were taken by surprise; he pounced on Quelch, threw an
arm round his neck from behind, and dragged him over on
his back on the sand.

There was a startled gasp from Quelch. Probably, in
the sudden surprise, he hardly knew what was happening to
him. Mug gave him no time to recover. He planted a
knee on him, and thievish hands ran through his pockets,
while Quelch sprawled and spluttered incoherently. An
unwashed hand came out of an inner pocket with an
envelope in it.

'Quick!' panted Harry Wharton.

Five fellows leaped out of cover, and rushed on the
scene. They came down the sloping beach like lightning
Mug jumped up, the envelope in his hand, and in another
moment he would have been running for the gully with his
prize, leaving Quelch to splutter. But in that moment, five
fellows, who seemed to the amazed Mug to have sprung
suddenly from nowhere, rushed him down, and he went
sprawling headlong on the sand. The envelope flew from
the unwashed hand, and Mug sprawled and yelled.

But it was only for a moment that he sprawled. His
career as a snapper-up of unconsidered trifles had made
Mug quick on the uptake. In a moment, he was on his feet
again, and running like a deer. He disappeared round a
bulging cliff, at a speed that would have done him credit on
the cinder-path, while Harry Wharton and Co. gathered
round their spluttering form-master, and Mr. Quelch sat up,
dizzily, and goggled at them.

CHAPTER 26

NO LUCK FOR COKER

'BLESS my soul!' gasped Mr. Quelch.

He sat on the sand, breathless.

Quelch, as a rule, was perfectly cool and collected. Seldom, or never, was the master of the Remove seen in a fluster. Even on the occasion when there had been a barring-out at Greyfriars, Quelch's calmness had not deserted him.

But for once, Quelch undoubtedly was in a fluster. That startling experience had quite upset him. Suddenly collared from behind, and dragged over on his back, it had seemed to Quelch as if earth and sky and sea were spinning around him. He gurgled for breath. He goggled at five members of his form as if they had been ghosts. He was quite incoherent.

'Bless my soul! What—what—who—what——' he stuttered. 'What—what—who—Is that you, Wharton? And you, Cherry? What—what—who was that man? What—what—what——?'

'I hope you're not hurt, sir——'

'Eh! What? Yes—no—bless my soul!'

'We saw him collar you, sir, and ran up——'

'What—who—where——?'

'He's gone, sir.'

'Bless my soul!'

'Please let us help you up, sir.'

Five fellows were quite concerned and sympathetic. All the more so, perhaps, because they were now caught out of bounds, with lines in the offing. It was possible that

Quelch, in the circumstances, might stretch a point in their favour. But while that hope was not absent, they were genuinely concerned for their form-master; and they helped him up, and helped his tottering steps back to his seat on the chalk rock, where he sat down again, still gasping for breath.

Gradually, Mr. Quelch recovered. He ceased, at last, to gasp. Nugent picked up his hat which had rolled away down the sands, and handed it to him, and Mr. Quelch replaced it on his head. Then he glanced round anxiously.

'My book!' he said.

He had dropped Horace, as well as his hat, in that sudden backward tumble. As he recovered, his thoughts ran, naturally, at once, to Quintus Horatius Flaccus. The juniors looked round, and Bob Cherry spotted Horace, and picked it up. That little volume, well-worn by thirty years or so in Quelch's pocket, safely restored.

'Thank you, Cherry!' said Mr. Quelch.

'Here's something else, sir!' said Harry. He picked up an envelope from the sand. 'That rascal pinched it from your pocket, and dropped it when we rushed him down.'

Mr. Quelch blinked at the envelope.

'What is that?' he asked. 'Oh! I remember! Thank you, Wharton! I should have been very sorry to lose that— it is something that Bunter asked me to mind for him! Thank you, my boy.'

'Oh!' gasped Harry.

The Famous Five exchanged glances. Quelch did not know what was in that envelope. They did!

That envelope was restored to Quelch's pocket. Quintus Horatius Flaccus followed it in. After that upset, it appeared that Quelch was no longer in a mood to peruse even the immortal Odes!

'Bless my soul!' said Mr. Quelch.   'No doubt that—that iniquitous ruffian—supposed that it was something of value!   Thank you, Wharton.   It would have been very unfortunate if I had lost that envelope, as I told Bunter that I would mind it for him.   Very unfortunate indeed!'   Mr. Quelch was calmer now.   'I must thank you boys for coming to my aid so promptly.'

'Not at all, sir!'

'Jolly glad we were here, sir.'

'Very glad to help, sir.'

'The gladfulness is terrific, esteemed sir.'

'But——!'   Mr. Quelch frowned.   'What are you doing here?   You are out of bounds here, Wharton.'

'Oh!   Yes—We—we——'

Quelch's frown intensified.   Evidently, he was recovering from the shock: and was himself again!

'School bounds are extended only on half-holidays,' he said, sternly.   'You are aware of that, Wharton.'

'Oh!   Yes, sir!'

'This is not a half-holiday.'

'Oh!   No, sir.'

'Then what does this mean?' rapped Mr. Quelch.

The juniors made no reply to that.   Really, no reply was needed: for it was quite clear what it meant: which was, that the Famous Five had either forgotten or disregarded bounds.   So, instead of replying, they looked as meekly penitent as they could.

However, Mr. Quelch's frown faded out.

Bounds, certainly, were bounds: but services rendered were services rendered!   It would have been somewhat ungracious to hand out penalties, to fellows who had shown up of their own accord, in coming to his aid.   There was a pause: but at length the severe countenance relaxed.

'Well, well,' said Mr. Quelch, after that pause. 'Never mind—never mind—I shall excuse you on this occasion. Go back to the school at once.'

'Yes, sir!'

'Thank you, sir.'

Johnny Bull cast a glance along the rugged line of cliffs. Mug Parkiss had disappeared, at top speed, in the direction of Friardale, the way the juniors had come.

'Perhaps you'd like us to stay, sir, in case that tramp came back!' suggested Johnny.

'What?' Quelch gave Johnny quite a freezing look. 'What? Do not be absurd, Bull! Go back to the school at once.'

'Oh! Yes, sir.'

Evidently, Quelch did not feel in need of further aid from those members of his form!

'Come on,' murmured Bob, hastily.

Happily relieved on the subject of 'lines', the Famous Five walked on towards the gully. They left their form-master sitting on the chalk rock, still breathing rather hard.

They tramped on to the gully, and turned into it, to clamber up to the cliff road above. It was a steep rugged slope between rocky walls. As they tramped up, a figure ahead of them came into view. It was that of Horace Coker, of the Greyfriars Fifth. Coker stared down at them as they came.

'Hallo, hallo, hallo! There's old Coker,' remarked Bob. 'He's out of bounds too. Better tip him that there's a beak about.'

Coker was staring hard at the Famous Five. He had seen nothing of what had happened on the beach, hidden from his view by the cliffs. At the sound of footsteps in the gully, he had expected to see Mug Parkiss returning: instead of which he beheld the much more pleasing countenances of the chums of the Remove. The sight of them however, did not seem to please Coker.

'Here, stop!' he rapped out, as the juniors came up, and they stopped.

'Ware beaks, Coker!' said Bob.

'Eh! What do you mean, you young ass?' snapped Coker.

'You're out of bounds——'

'Don't be cheeky!'

'There's a beak on the beach,' explained Bob. 'Our beak! If he spots you he might mention it to Prout.'

'I've told you not to be cheeky, Cherry.' Coker was not in need of wise counsel from juniors! 'I know Quelch is on the beach. What the dickens were you young scallywags doing there, out of bounds?'

'No more out of bounds than you are, Coker,' grunted Johnny Bull.

'If you cheek me, Bull——'

'Oh, rats!' said Johnny.

'Order!' exclaimed Bob Cherry. Bob was still mindful of that rescue in Friardale Wood, and anxious to steer clear of trouble with the rescuer. 'Put a sock in it, Johnny. We've been on a ramble along the beach, Coker. Anything else you'd like to know?'

'You've seen Quelch?' asked Coker.

'Yes: as large as life, and twice as natural.'

'Don't be a young ass, Cherry! Did you see anybody else?' Coker seemed anxious for information: why, the juniors could not imagine. They were not likely to guess Coker's interest in Mr. Parkiss.

'Oh, yes, that frowsy tramp you punched in the wood on Monday,' answered Bob.

'Oh!   Hanging about, I suppose?' said Coker, casually.
Bob Cherry chuckled.

'Not exactly,' he answered.   'You couldn't see his heels
for dust, the last we saw of him.'

Coker started.

'What?   What do you mean?' he exclaimed.

'You see, he went for Quelch and we barged in,'
explained Bob.   'He was going through Quelch's pockets,
but we stopped him——'

'You stopped him?' gasped Coker.

'What do you think?' said Bob.   'We'd jolly well have
given him toco, too, only he got away so quickly, and ran
for it, and——'

'You silly young jackanapes——'

'Eh?'

'You blithering young nitwit——'

'What?'

The fabled basilisk could hardly have equalled the glare
that Horace Coker gave the Famous Five.   They gazed at
him in astonishment.   They were very far from guessing
that, by coming to their form-master's aid so promptly, they
had disconcerted a deep-laid scheme of Horace Coker's.

'You—you—you——!' hooted Coker.   He seemed at a
loss for sufficiently expressive words.   'You—you—you—
you—oh, take that!'

'Oh!' roared Bob.   It came so suddenly that he had no
choice about taking it.   It was a hefty smack that made his
head ring.

'And that——!' added Coker.   Evidently, he was going
on with the good work!   But he was given no time.

The Famous Five jumped at him as one man.   Coker
rolled over in their grasp, and came down with a heavy
bump on hard chalk.

'Oh!' gasped Bob, rubbing his head. 'The mad ass—what the dickens—scrag him! Roll him over!'

'Scrag him terrifically.'

Why Horace Coker had erupted like a sudden volcano, in that unexpected and extraordinary manner, the chums of the Remove did not know. But they were prompt to react: and reacted with energy.

Coker of the Fifth was a hefty man to handle. But five juniors were equal to the task. They handled him quite effectively. For several minutes, 'beans' were administered to Horace Coker. It was in fact quite a bean-feast for him. Then the Famous Five, a little breathless after their exertions, went on up the gully—leaving Coker horizontal and quite breathless.

When they looked back from the top of the gully, they had a view of Coker sitting up, gasping for breath, and rubbing various places that appeared damaged. They waved their hands to him in smiling farewell, and went cheerily on their way.

CHAPTER 27

THE LIMIT

'BUNTER!'

'Oh, lor'!'

'What? What did you say, Bunter?'

'Oh! I—I—I said yes, sir!' gasped Billy Bunter.

Mr. Quelch was not the person Bunter desired to meet, at that moment. When he rolled out of the House after dinner, he was looking for Coker of the Fifth. Dinner at the Remove table was quite good and quite ample—ample for any fellow but William George Bunter. But though the fat Owl annexed as many helpings as were practicable under a gimlet-eye, there was still available cargo-space within his wide circumference: and Bunter liked to load up to the Plimsoll line, and a little over.

Had his celebrated postal-order arrived, Bunter would have headed for the school shop. But it hadn't. So he was looking for Coker. But as he rolled out, he met, not Horace Coker, but Henry Samuel Quelch. Reluctantly, he had to stop, at his master's voice. Quelch gave him a frown.

'Your lines have not been brought to me, Bunter!' he rapped.

'Oh! Yes! No! I—I mean, I—I forgot——!' stammered Bunter.

'Have you written them, Bunter?'

'Oh! Yes, sir! I—I mean, no, sir! I—I was just going to, sir——'

'I recommend you to do so without further delay,

Bunter,' said Mr. Quelch, grimly. 'For if you do not hand them to me when you go into form this afternoon, I shall cane you.'

With that, Mr. Quelch walked on.

Billy Bunter blinked after him, with an expressive blink. He had not time now to look for Coker, and extract what he called a 'quip prop quop' from that long-suffering Fifth-form man. Quelch wanted his lines, and Quelch was not to be denied.

Those lines had haunted Bunter. They had been awarded on Monday, and now it was Friday. Non-delivery had caused them to be doubled. Further non-delivery had caused them to be trebled. If Quelch had kept on at that game, doubling and trebling ad lib., Bunter wouldn't have minded. But trebling was the limit: after that it was 'whops'. Billy Bunter now had to produce three hundred lines when the Remove went into form: or else——!

Certainly there was time, between tiffin and form, for an industrious fellow to grind out even three hundred Latin lines. But Billy Bunter was not an industrious fellow. He was quite the reverse of an industrious fellow. The prospect, to Bunter, was quite appalling.

'Oh, lor'!' groaned Bunter.

He was quite keen to look for Coker of the Fifth, and extract from him a 'quip prop quop' in the shape of tarts at the tuck-shop. He was not in the least keen to go up to his study and transcribe the deathless verse of Virgil. But those lines had to be done, unless Quelch's cane was to contact his ample trousers.

'Beast!' moaned Bunter. His fat face registered dismal dismay and despondency.

'Hallo, hallo, hallo! Enjoying life, old fat man?'
came a cheery voice.

Billy Bunter blinked round. The Famous Five had
come out of the House, in a cheery bunch. Bunter's blink
at them was far from cheery.

'I say, you fellows, Quelch has just asked me for my
lines——' mumbled Bunter. 'I say, there's three hundred,
and it's going to be 'whops' if I don't take them in when we
go into form.'

'Why haven't you done them, then?' asked Bob.

'Well, I haven't had time——'

'Too busy sticking Coker for tuck?' asked Johnny Bull,
sarcastically.

'Oh really, Bull——'

'Better get going on them, you fat ass,' said Harry
Wharton. 'You've plenty of time before form, if you
buck up.'

'I—I say, you fellows, suppose you help?' suggested
Bunter. 'It's an awful lot, you know. You could make
your fist near enough to mine, for Quelch, couldn't you?'

'Easy!' assented Bob. 'We should only have to make
the lines look as if a spider had done them, crawling out of
an inkpot.'

'Ha, ha, ha!'

'Beast! I—I mean, look here, old chap, you help a
fellow out,' pleaded Bunter. 'Three hundred, you know!
If you chaps do forty each, I'll do the other fifty——'

'Ha, ha, ha!'

'What are you cackling at?' hooted Bunter, indignantly.
'Think it's funny for a fellow to be stuck with three hundred
lines? Look here, you do forty each, and I'll jolly well
stand you a spread after class—what about that?'

'In Coker's study?' grinned Bob.

'You fat villain!' said Johnny Bull.

'You pernicious porpoise!' said Frank Nugent.

'You terrific toad!' said Hurree Jamset Ram Singh.

'Well, Coker wouldn't say no, you can bank on that,' said Bunter. 'I've jolly well got him feeding from my hand, I can tell you. You won't see him smacking my head again. More likely you'll see me smacking his! He, he, he! I can tell you Coker has to jump when I say jump! Oh, crikey!' added Bunter, as a quite bright idea came into his fat head. 'If you fellows won't help me out with my lines for Quelch——'

'No "if" about that!' assured Bob.

'Well, I'll jolly well ask Coker to do them, then——'

'Oh, my hat! I can see Coker doing lines for a Remove man!' ejaculated Bob. 'Better guard with your left when you ask him!'

'Well, I jolly well shan't ask him—I shall jolly well tell him, and you'll see!' snorted Bunter. And he rolled away, once more in search of Horace Coker.

The Famous Five stared after him, as he rolled.

'By gum!' said Bob Cherry, with a deep breath. 'That's the jolly old limit, if that fat villain makes Coker do his lines for him.'

'Coker wouldn't!' said Frank Nugent, shaking his head.

'He can't help himself. Hallo, hallo, hallo, there he is now,' said Bob. 'Poor old Coker—I'll bet he wishes by this time that he hadn't started doing limericks about his beak.'

Coker of the Fifth came out of the House. He walked into the quad with his usual aspect, as if the quadrangle and the rest of Greyfriars belonged to him. But a change came over him, as he saw Bunter.

M

He stopped in his lofty stride. He hesitated. Then he turned, to go back into the House.

Harry Wharton and Co. exchanged glances. Coker, actually, was dodging Bunter—the lofty, truculent Horace was dodging the Owl of the Remove! Thus were the mighty fallen!

Unluckily for Coker, a pair of little round eyes, and a pair of big round spectacles, spotted him. Bunter's fat squeak was heard.

'I say, Coker!'

The Famous Five watched, with interest. Coker, affecting not to hear the fat squeak, walked quickly towards the doorway. Billy Bunter rolled after him.

'Here, Coker!' shouted Bunter.

Not only the Famous Five, but a dozen or more other fellows, looked round. Coker's face crimsoned. He walked on still more quickly.

'Coker! Stop!' roared Bunter.

Coker stopped.

Billy Bunter rolled up, and joined him. He gave him an indignant blink.

'Look here, you jolly well stop when I call you, Coker!' snapped Bunter. 'I don't want any swank from you, I can tell you.'

Coker seemed on the point of choking.

'What do you want?' he breathed.

'Come into the House——'

'I—I'm not going in just now——'

'I said come into the House.'

Coker gave him a look. Then he went quietly into the House with Bunter. The Famous Five exchanged glances again. Evidently, as he had declared, that 'bad lad'

Bunter had Coker feeding from his hand! Bob knitted his brows.

'That's got to stop, you men,' he said.

To which his comrades assented: but the question still was 'how'. It was Bob who, after considerable cogitation, propounded the 'how'.

CHAPTER 28

HARD LINES!

'PRIME!' said Potter.

'Topping!' agreed Greene.

The subject of those remarks was a large bag of cherries, on the table in the Fifth-form study. Potter and Greene were helping themselves from that bag, with considerable satisfaction. Those cherries were, undoubtedly, prime and topping. Coker, who had plenty of money to splash about, always had the best.

They were Coker's cherries: but Coker had not come up to the study to sample them: he had gone out after dinner. His friends did not miss him. They felt quite equal to dealing with that bag, without Coker's aid. And there was one good point about old Horace: he wouldn't have minded a bit if they had wolfed the lot! Which they looked like doing!

But that cherry-ripe feast was interrupted, by footsteps in the passage, and the sound of a fat voice.

'Come on, Coker!'

'Look here, Bunter——'

'I said come on!'

'Oh, all right!'

Potter and Greene ceased, for a moment, operations on the cherries, and exchanged an eloquent glance. Coker was, after all, coming up to the study, and apparently that fat Remove tick was with him. Potter and Greene were glad to remember that they had booted Bunter the previous day. Gladly they would have booted him again.

174

Coker tramped into the study, with knitted brows.
After him rolled Billy Bunter. The fat Owl gave the two
seniors at the table a wary blink. He had not forgotten his
experience in that study the day before. But it was all right
with Coker present. Coker had to see him through. The
hapless Horace had no choice about that.

Bunter's second blink was at the bag of cherries. His
fat face brightened. Bunter liked cherries.

'I say, you fellows, I'll have some of those!' said Bunter,
cheerfully: and he extended a fat paw to the bag.

'You cheeky fat tick!' breathed Potter.

'Get out!' hissed Greene.

'Oh, all right,' said Bunter. 'If Coker doesn't want me
here, I'll go fast enough. I've got to see my beak and ask
him for something he's minding for me, Coker——'

Coker gave Potter and Greene a gloomy glare.

'For goodness sake, pack it up, you fellows,' he snapped,
irritably. 'Bunter can stick here if he likes.'

Potter and Greene rose from the table, as Bunter's fat
paw was inserted into the bag of cherries. Those cherries
might be both prime and topping: but there was a limit.
They were not standing this.

'Come on, Greeney,' said Potter. 'Let's get out of this.'

'Let's!' agreed Greene. 'You can have your fag friends
all to yourself, Coker.'

And they walked out of the study: two distinct sniffs
floating back as they went.

Coker hardly heeded them. He stood looking at
Bunter, who had taken the chair vacated by Potter, and was
busy on the cherries.

'Well?' rapped Coker, at last, as the fat Owl seemed too
busy to speak. 'What is it you want, Bunter?'

'Oh!' Bunter's fat voice came a little muffled by a

mouthful of cherries. 'It's about my lines, Coker. I've got three hundred from Quelch, to hand in when we go into form.'

'What about it?' snapped Coker.

'I thought you'd like to help me with them, old chap.'

'Old chap' from Bunter made Horace Coker clench his fists convulsively. But he unclenched them again. A few days ago, a hefty smack on a fat head would have been Coker's rejoinder to such cheek. But with every passing day, Coker realized more and more clearly that he dared not let that limerick come to light. The bare thought of seeing it pinned up on the board, for all the school to read, made him feel quite faint. Like Lucifer, Son of the Morning, Coker had fallen from his high estate, and great was the fall thereof!

'Get out some impot paper, will you?' went on Bunter. 'Don't stand there doing nothing.'

'You cheeky little fat freak!' gasped Coker. He made a stride towards Bunter. Just for a moment, it seemed to him that even the inevitable interview with the Head, and the 'sack', would be better than this!

But it was only for a moment!

He made only one stride. Then he stopped. Bunter blinked at him.

'That will do, Coker!' he snapped. 'Get some impot paper. There's no time for you to loaf about.'

How Horace Coker suppressed his feelings, he really did not know. But somehow he did suppress them. In silence, he sorted out impot paper from the table drawer, while Bunter guzzled cherries.

'You've got a Virgil here, I suppose,' said Bunter.

'Yes,' breathed Coker.

'Open it at the second book.'

Coker opened the Aeneid at Liber II.

'I'm going to do the first page,' explained Bunter. 'Can't be too careful with Quelch. I'll begin at "conticuere omnes", see? Mind, I'll do a whole page. You'll do the rest, won't you, old fellow?'

'Look here——!' breathed Coker.

'No time to talk,' interrupted Bunter. 'Those lines have got to be done. Mind you make your fist look like mine. I don't want Quelch to smell a rat. Let's look at that Virgil!' Bunter blinked at the Aeneid. 'Let's see—I'll make it twenty lines in my lot. You begin at "Est in conspectu Tenedos", see?'

Billy Bunter resumed operations on the cherries.

Coker stood looking at him, for a long moment. Was even the 'sack' worse than taking orders from a cheeky, grubby fag? Actually, it was: and Coker had to make the best of it. Sitting in his study grinding out lines for that cheeky fat smudge was awful. But to hear the gates of Greyfriars School close behind him for the last time would be, so to speak, awfuller! In suffocated silence, Coker sat down at the table, and began to transcribe Virgil.

He had two hundred and eighty lines to write, from 'Est in conspectu Tenedos' to 'arboribusque ontecta recessit'. Even Bunter realized that he had better do the beginning of that imposition, to meet the gimlet-eyes. For the rest, Coker's fist was not unlike Bunter's: both were irregular scrawls. It was not unknown for fellows to help one another out with lines: though assuredly aid had never been more reluctantly given than on the present occasion.

Coker scribbled and scribbled and scribbled, while Billy Bunter operated on the bag of cherries, till not a single cherry was left in the bag. Then the fat junior started on his section of the impot: from 'conticuere omnes' to 'armato milite complent'.

Coker was still grinding wearily at his two hundred and eighty, when Bunter had finished his twenty. The fat Owl blinked across the table at him.

'How many more have you got to do, Coker?' he inquired.

'About seventy more,' breathed Coker.

'Well, buck up! They've got to be finished before form.'

'Look here, Bunter——'

'Don't jaw, old chap—just get on with it.'

With really remarkable self-control, Coker refrained from hurling the inkpot at Bunter, and got on with it. Billy Bunter transferred his plump person to the armchair, where he stretched out little fat legs, and leaned a fat head back on a cushion, in lazy comfort.

There was a cheery grin on his fat face. This, from Bunter's point of view, was distinctly good. More and more it was dawning on his fat brain what a valuable possession that limerick was. Lines from Quelch—which often came Bunter's way—were not going to be such a spot of bother as formerly—Coker was going to do them for him, so long as he had that limerick. It was quite a cheery prospect.

Coker scribbled on, with feelings growing deeper and deeper. The lines were finished at last. It was almost time for class when Coker was through.

Then Billy Bunter detached himself from the armchair. With a grinning fat face, he placed the sheets together: his own twenty lines coming first to meet the gimlet-eye's first glance. The rest, Bunter hoped at least, would pass muster at Quelch's second glance. There was really not a lot of difference between one inky scrawl and another.

'Thanks, old fellow,' said Bunter, affably.

And he rolled out of Coker's study with his completed impot. Coker was left in a boiling state—almost boiling over.

CHAPTER 29

BEND OVER, BUNTER

'HALLO, hallo! hallo!'

'Hold on, Bunter.'

'Waiting for you, old fat man.'

Billy Bunter blinked at the Famous Five. Why they were waiting for him, when he rolled out on the landing from the Fifth-form studies, he did not know. But there they were—waiting.

Bunter had to hold on. With five smiling juniors blocking his way to the stairs, he had no choice about that.

'I say, you fellows, no larks!' squeaked the fat Owl. 'The bell will be going in a minute or two.'

'Ten minutes yet,' said Bob Cherry, cheerfully. 'Lots of time, old fat frump. Is that your impot for Quelch?'

'Eh? Yes. Look here, let a fellow pass,' snapped Bunter. 'I'm not going to be late for class. Gerrout of the way, will you?'

'Come along with us——!'

'Oh!' Bunter's expression changed. 'If it's a feed, all right. Is it a feed?'

'Not exactly a feed,' said Bob. 'It's a sort of burnt offering that we've got in mind. Come along.'

'What the dickens do you mean—a burnt offering?' snapped Bunter.

'You'll see! Come on,' said Harry Wharton.

As the Famous Five gathered round him, and Bob took one fat arm, and Johnny Bull another, Billy Bunter had to 'come on'. He came on unwillingly, but he came. The

Famous Five walked him into the Remove passage, and stopped at No. 1 Study. They walked him into that study.

Harry Wharton closed the door. That proceeding caused the fat Owl to cast an alarmed blink round at five smiling faces.

'I say, you fellows, wharrer you up to?' squeaked Bunter. 'Look here, we've jolly well got to go down to the form-room——'

'Hand over that impot,' said Bob.

'Eh! What for?'

'Just because I tell you to. Sharp.'

'Shan't!' howled Bunter. 'Wharrer you mean? You ain't going to lark with my lines. It's whops if I don't hand them in to Quelch when we go in.'

'Are you handing them over?'

'No, I jolly well ain't,' hooted Bunter.

'Kick him, Franky.'

'Yaroooh!'

One contact with Frank Nugent's foot seemed enough for Bunter. He handed over the imposition.

Bob Cherry examined it.

'How much of this is yours?' he asked. 'Blessed if I can tell one scrawl from another! How much did you do?'

'Twenty,' yapped Bunter. 'Now you give me my impot. What the dickens do you want to squint at it for?'

Bob detached the top sheet, written in Bunter's own 'fist', and with 'W. G. Bunter' written in the top left-hand corner, according to rule. He handed that single sheet back to the fat Owl.

'That's yours, then,' he said. 'You can keep it, and show it up to Quelch.'

'Wharrer you mean?' howled Bunter. 'I've got to show up three hundred lines.'

'Rather a pity that you haven't written them, then,' said Bob, affably. 'Next time, you'd better get going and not leave it so late.'

'Procrastination is the long lane that has no turning, as the English proverb remarks, my esteemed Bunter,' grinned Hurree Jamset Ram Singh.

'Gimme my lines!' yelled Bunter.

'You've got them——'

'Ha, ha, ha!'

'Gimme the rest, you beast——'

'The rest are Coker's!' said Bob. 'That's where the burnt offering comes in. Get the idea? We can't stop you sticking that Fifth-form fathead for tuck—but we can jolly well stop you landing your lines on him. You've got your own twenty lines. Coker's are going up in smoke.'

'What?' gasped Bunter.

'Got a match, anybody?' asked Bob.

'Here you are!' Johnny Bull produced a match-box.

Bob crossed to the fireplace. He jammed the sheets covered by Coker's scrawl into the grate. Billy Bunter's eyes almost popped through his spectacles as he watched him.

He understood now what Bob meant by a 'burnt offering'. Two hundred and eighty lines, scrawled in Coker's study, were going up in smoke! Bunter's own lines were safe in his fat hands. Coker's were going to be consumed in the grate in No. 1 Study. Three hundred lines, happily completed in time to save the fat Owl from 'whops', were to be reduced, at one fell swoop, to twenty!

'Stop!' yelled Bunter, frantically.

Bob scratched a match.

'Will you stop?' shrieked Bunter. 'I tell you it will be whops if I don't take those lines into form.'

'Anybody going to weep briny tears if that fat villain gets whops?' inquired Bob Cherry.

'Ha, ha, ha!'

The chums of the Remove certainly did not look like shedding briny tears over Billy Bunter's woes. They were all laughing.

Bob applied the match to the impot papers in the grate. In sheer desperation, the fat Owl rushed at him, and grabbed his arm.

'Stop it!' he yelled.

'Kick him, Johnny.'

'Pleased!' said Johnny, and he did.

'Ow! Beast! wow! I—I say, you fellows, gimme my lines! I say, it will be "whops" from Quelch if I don't take them in! I say—oh, crikey!'

There was a flutter of flame in the grate. Two hundred and eighty Latin lines blazed up, and disappeared in smoke.

'Beasts!' groaned Bunter.

'That's that!' said Bob. 'And now listen to this, you fat, frowsy, unscrupulous porpoise. We're going to keep an eye on you after this, and if you ever get Coker to do lines for you again, they'll go the same way, and we'll boot you into the bargain. Got that?'

'Beast!'

'Hallo, hallo, hallo! There's the bell!'

'Come on, you fellows.'

The Famous Five crowded out of the study. Billy Bunter was left with a single sheet in his fat hand, gazing mournfully at a little pile of black ashes in the grate. The bell was ringing, and there certainly was no time now for Bunter to write his lines, if he had felt so disposed. It was going to be 'whops'.

'Beasts!' groaned Bunter.

He rolled out of the study, a sad and sorrowful Owl. His fat face was lugubrious, as he joined the Remove at the form-room door. He had twenty lines to show up, instead of three hundred! The outcome was not doubtful! Five fellows smiled at him: receiving in return a glare that might almost have cracked Bunter's spectacles.

Mr. Quelch's *eye* singled out Bunter at once when he let in his form.

'Bunter!'

'Yes, sir!' mumbled Bunter.

'You may place your lines on my desk.'

A dispirited Owl placed a single sheet on the desk. Mr. Quelch glanced at it. Then the gimlet-eyes fixed on Bunter.

'There are twenty lines here, Bunter. What does this mean?'

'I—I—I——!' mumbled Bunter.

'You have not written your imposition, Bunter, after what I said to you on the subject!' Mr. Quelch picked up his cane. 'You will bend over, Bunter.'

'I—I—I——'

'Bend over, Bunter!'

'Oh, lor'!'

Whop! whop! whop!

'Ow! wow! wow!'

'Go to your place, Bunter. I shall expect the remainder of your lines tomorrow,' snapped Mr. Quelch. 'If they are not handed to me by tea-time tomorrow, Bunter, I warn you that I shall deal with you more severely. I will not permit such idleness and procrastination in my form, Bunter. Go to your place.'

An unhappy Owl wriggled through that lesson.

CHAPTER 30

IN AMBUSH

'BRACE up, old man.'

Potter and Greene gave that advice.

Coker did not heed it. He did not look either like bracing up or smiling. Indeed, his gloomy and pessimistic countenance seemed to indicate that he was bent on under-studying that ancient monarch who never smiled again.

Potter and Greene were cheerful enough. The three of them were following the footpath through Friardale Wood. They had tickets for the Regal at Pegg—Coker's tickets, of course—and leave from their form-master: and a visit to the pictures after class, with tea at the Regal to follow, seemed to Potter and Greene a quite cheerful proposition. Potter and Greene were quite prepared to enjoy themselves. But Coker's gloomy looks were rather a damper.

In point of fact, Potter and Greene were getting a little fed up with Coker and his peck of troubles.

No doubt they sympathized with a fellow placed in so peculiar a predicament. On the other hand, if a fellow asked for trouble, he couldn't reasonably complain if trouble accrued. A fellow shouldn't write disrespectful limericks about his beak, to begin with. And if he did, he should take jolly good care not to strew them about the quad for anybody to pick up. And if a fellow did pick them up, he shouldn't smack that fellow's head and put his back up. It was all Coker's own fault, from beginning to end. And the result was that Potter and Greene had to tolerate a fat grubby fag having the run of the study: and

Coker looking and behaving like a bear with a sore head!
Even now, on the way to the Regal, he was looking more
like a fellow going into Extra School than a fellow going to
the pictures.

Coker tramped on in glum silence.

Potter and Greene did not exactly want conversation
from Coker. They had more than enough of that, as a
rule. Indeed, it often seemed to them that silence was never
so golden as when Coker left off talking. All the same,
this glum and gloomy pessimism was a damper.

Really, they would have preferred to leave Coker behind,
when they walked over to the Regal at Pegg. But as Coker
had the tickets, that was scarcely practicable.

'Jolly good picture at the Regal, I heard from Hilton,'
Potter remarked.

Grunt, from Coker.

'It's jolly rotten,' he said, breaking silence at last.

'Is it?' said Potter. 'Hilton said it was good—he's
seen it——'

'Oh, don't be an ass!' snapped Coker. 'I'm not talking
about pictures.'

'I was!' said Potter.

'You would be!' said Coker, with scorn. 'Pontius Pilate
fiddling while Carthage was burning hadn't a thing on you
fellows. Fat lot you care about a chap having the sword of
Sophocles hanging over his head.

Coker's frown deepened.

'It's too jolly rotten,' he went on. 'I've got to get that
limerick from Quelch—somehow! I tell you I've got to!
I had to do Bunter's lines for him this afternoon. What
could a fellow do, when he's only got to stick that limerick
up on the board, and it's the long jump for me? I tell you,
I've got to get hold of that dashed limerick! But how?'

His friends made no reply to that.   No more than Coker did they know 'how'.   They refrained from telling him that they wished he wouldn't keep on harping on the subject of that limerick!   They walked on in silence.

Potter and Greene were thinking of the Regal, the pictures, and tea.   Coker was trying to think of some way out of that awful 'jam'.

But Horace Coker's rather solid brain was not very useful for thinking purposes.   He was ready to take almost any step to recover possession of that limerick.   But he could not think of one to take.   He had perhaps a faint hope that Mug Parkiss, hanging about with an eye open for Mr. Quelch, might have better luck at a second go.   But that hope was very faint.   And so long as that limerick remained in Quelch's pocket, Coker had to remain under a fat and grubby thumb!

Deep in thought, Coker walked very slowly.   Pictures at the Regal did not interest him as they did Potter and Greene.   He did not care two hoots, or one, whether they were late for the picture or not.

Potter and Greene, naturally, did.   It was not for the pleasure of Coker's company that they were walking through Friardale Wood.   They exchanged glances of growing impatience across Coker.

'Better buck up a bit, Coker,' said Potter, at last.

'Eh!'   Coker jerked out of deep cogitation.   'What?'

'We shall be late for the big picture, at this rate.'

'Bother the big picture,' said Coker, irritably.   'Blow the big picture!'

'Well, it's no good being late, if we're going at all,' said Potter, tartly.

'Oh, don't jaw.'

'Look here——!' began Greene.

N

'I said don't jaw.'

Only that fact that the tickets were in Coker's pocket, restrained Potter and Greene, at that moment, from telling him what they thought of him. They gave one another eloquent looks.

A few minutes later, Potter rather ostentatiously looked at his watch.

'None too much time now,' he said.

'We're going to be late, Coker,' said Greene.

'Oh, rot!' said Coker. 'It's hours yet to lock-ups. What do you mean?'

'I don't mean lock-ups—I mean at the Regal——'

Coker came to an exasperated halt.

'Blow the Regal!' he hooted. 'Dash the Regal! Look here, you fellows cut on, if you're so anxious about a silly picture, and give a fellow a rest.'

'Oh, all right,' said Potter. 'But——'

'Don't jaw.'

'But——!' said Greene.

'For goodness sake, don't butt like a pair of billy-goats! If you're in a hurry, cut on, I tell you.'

'Yes, but——!' said Potter and Greene together.

'But—but—but——!' mimicked Coker. 'I said cut on, if you're in a hurry. Nothing to but about, that I know of.'

'But you've got the tickets!' yelled Potter.

'Oh!' Coker had forgotten, in his stress of mind, that trifling circumstance. 'Oh! The tickets! Why couldn't you say so, instead of jawing and jawing and jawing and jawing? Here they are! Now cut on, and give a fellow a chance to think when he's in a jam!'

Potter and Greene were quite content to cut on—with the tickets! If Coker fancied that they wanted his company as well as the tickets, it was only one more of Coker's many mistakes. They cut on quite cheerfully, leaving Coker to follow, or not, as the spirit might move him.

They disappeared up the footpath.

Coker, in fact, was in no mood for pictures. It mattered nothing to him whether he arrived at the Regal early or late. He tramped on slowly, his hands driven deep into his pockets, his brow corrugated. How was he going to get out of that awful jam? How?

He heard without heeding, a sound of running feet on the footpath behind him. But as those hurried footsteps came nearer, he gave a grunt, and stepped to the side of the path, glancing back. The footpath was narrow and winding, and shaded by leafy branches. Someone was coming on at a rapid run, not yet in sight: and Coker did not want that someone to crash into him. So he stepped aside, casting a frowning glance back.

Then a running figure came in sight, round a wind of the path.

Coker gave a start, as he saw it. He knew at once the unwashed, stubbly face under the battered hat.

'Him!' grunted Coker.

Why Mug Parkiss was running, at such a pace, under the shady branches, was not clear. He was not in much of a condition for a race. Beer and tobacco did not make for fitness. Mug was panting, and his unwashed face perspired. But he was evidently in a hurry, and he came on fast.

But he halted suddenly, at the sight of Horace Coker.

'Oh! You, guvnor!' ejaculated Mug.

'In a hurry?' asked Coker, sarcastically. 'Is there a bobby after you?'

'No, there ain't, guvnor. But you can 'ave that quid ready,' answered Mug. 'It was bad luck last time, down on the beach, because of them dratted schoolboys, but it's okay this time.'

'What do you mean?' grunted Coker.

Mug cast a backward glance, and then approached him, breathlessly.

'I been keeping an eye open for that bony old gent,' he explained. 'He's coming through the wood now.'

'Oh!' exclaimed Coker.

'I jest cut ahead, to lay for him!' panted Mug. 'Safer 'ere, in the middle of the wood, guvnor. I tell you, that bony old party is going to walk right into my 'ands this time, and I'll 'ave that letter you want off him, afore he knows what's 'appening to 'im.'

'Oh!' repeated Coker. His look was eager now. Mug, it appeared, had spotted Mr. Quelch on one of his walks abroad, and had seen him turn into that footpath from Friardale Lane. With great cunning, Mug had cut ahead, to 'lay' for the 'bony old gent' in a lonely spot.

'He won't be long arter me,' went on Mug. 'He covers the ground, that bony old gent does, with them long legs of his'n. But I got time to pick a spot. It's okay this time, guvnor.'

Coker nodded. These, even Coker realized, were rather desperate measures. But he had to have that limerick!

'Mind, no rough stuff!' he said, warningly. 'You can tip him up, but if you hurt him, I'll jolly well make mince-meat of you. Mind, I mean that.'

'Don't you worry, guvnor! I wouldn't 'urt a 'air of his blinking 'ead,' assured Mug. 'I jest tips him over and grabs that letter and scrams—the bony old party will 'ardly know what's 'appened.'

'All right, then,' said Coker. 'I'll keep out of sight. If you get that envelope, there's a quid ready for you.'

Coker backed into the trees, one side of the footpath. Mug Parkiss backed into a thicket on the other side.

The footpath was left deserted.

Coker, peering from behind a tree, could see nothing of Mug. Obviously, Quelch would see nothing of him when he came along. A sudden rush from the tramp would do the trick: and this time there were no members of Mr. Quelch's form at hand to barge in. All, at last, was going well: that limerick was coming back to its owner: and then all that Coker had to do was to walk back to the school, look for Billy Bunter, and administer the booting that that bad lad so richly deserved. It was quite a cheery prospect.

On either side of the leafy footpath, they waited: listening for the sound of approaching footsteps, waiting for Mr. Quelch to walk into the ambush. And a few minutes later, Mr. Quelch walked into it!

CHAPTER 31

JUST LIKE COKER

'OH!' gasped Mr. Quelch.

He had been taken by surprise on the beach the previous day. Now he was taken by surprise again. A schoolmaster, walking sedately along a leafy footpath in a shady wood, naturally did not expect a tattered figure to shoot suddenly out of a thicket, crash into him, and knock him spinning. That, to Mr. Quelch's great surprise, was what happened.

Quelch went over like a skittle.

Coker, behind his tree, knitted his brows. He had warned Mug against the 'rough stuff'. But he had to admit that this was a little rough. Still it was, after all, only a tumble, and he had to have that limerick! It would be over in a few moments, anyway.

But in that view, Coker was in error. It was not by any means over in a few moments. Mug Parkiss flung himself on the Remove master as he sprawled in the grass, groping for a pocket. He did not expect trouble from that 'bony old party'. So Mug was surprised, in his turn, when the bony old party lashed up at him with a rather bony fist, catching him fairly in the eye.

'Oooh!' spluttered Mug.

'Scoundrel!' panted Mr. Quelch.

Quelch, of course, could only suppose that the tramp was a footpad, bent on robbery. He knew him at once as the man on the beach the day before. This time, though, taken by surprise, he was prompt to react. Mug would never have dreamed that so bony an old party packed so effective a punch. He learned it, as Quelch's knuckles banged into his eye. He reeled back from that bang.

Instead of pinning Quelch down, and going through his pockets, as planned, Mug sat down suddenly in the grass beside him.

Quelch struggled up, to his knees.

'Cor'!' gasped Mug. He blinked with a half-closed eye, and his unwashed face registered fury. Mug was hurt: and he forgot all about Coker's stern injunctions respecting the 'rough stuff'.

He hurled himself at Quelch.

Before the Remove master could get on his feet, Mug was upon him again, grasping him and wrenching him over. Quelch, undaunted, struck again, and yet again, and both punches crashed hard in an unwashed face. They came back with interest, the enraged ruffian raining blows.

Coker, behind his tree, peered at the scene, almost spell-bound with horror. He had never expected or dreamed of anything like this. Really, he might have: but he hadn't.

For a moment or two, spell-bound, he stared. Then he rushed out into the footpath.

His limerick, and the sword of Damocles hanging over his head, were quite forgotten now. The sight of an elderly gentleman, a master at his own school, struggling under a rain of blows, banished everything else from Coker's mind. He rushed on the scene, and Mug, as he rained blows, received an unexpected crash on the side of his tousled head.

'You rotten brute!' roared Coker. 'Take that—and that—and that—and that—and that——'

Mug yelled frantically as he took them.

'And that—and that——'

'Oooh! Ow! Keep orf!' shrieked Mug. 'Oh, my eye! Oh, gosh! Oooh! Woooh!'

He jumped back, and back, under Coker's onslaught. Coker followed him up, still hitting. Mug, in desperation, hit out fiercely in return.

Mr. Quelch staggered up. He blinked dizzily at the scene. Quelch had had some hard knocks, before Coker intervened. He was a little dazed, and quite breathless. Dizzily, he watched that hectic combat, panting for breath.

It did not last long.

Coker had landed about a dozen good ones, when a final terrific punch laid Mug Parkiss on his back in the grass. He stayed there.

Coker glared down at him.

'Get up, and have some more!' he roared.

'Ow! Ooogh! Ow!' moaned Mug. 'You keep orf! Blow you, keep orf, can't you? Ow! My eye! Wow! My boko! Ow! Oooh!'

'Coker!' gasped Mr. Quelch.

Coker looked round at him.

'It's all right sir!' I'll jolly well give this brute a jolly good hiding——' he said. 'He hasn't had half enough yet.'

In that opinion, Mr. Parkiss evidently did not concur. He squirmed away, picked himself up, and started to run. Coker rushed after him. His foot shot out, and landed with a crash on tattered trousers. Yelling, Mr. Parkiss fled up the footpath and vanished.

'Coker!' gasped Mr. Quelch, again.

Coker turned back, rather reluctantly. He would gladly have given Mug some more. However, he turned back.

'Not hurt, I hope, sir,' said Coker. Somehow or other, during those hectic moments, Coker seemed to have forgotten that it was he, Horace James Coker, who had set the

HIS LAST CHANCE WAS GONE.

tramp on, in the first place.   But he remembered it now, and
he felt, and looked, somewhat shamefaced.

'A—a— little,' said Mr. Quelch.   'I should certainly
have been severely hurt, Coker, but for your aid.   Thank
you, Coker.'

'Oh!   Not at all, sir!' stammered Coker.   'I'm sorry—
I—I—I mean, I—I couldn't stand that brute pitching into
you like that, sir!   I wish I'd given him a few more, now.'

'I shall not continue my walk,' said Mr. Quelch.   'Thank
you once more, Coker—I am very much obliged to you.'

With that, Mr. Quelch turned, to retrace his steps.   He
did not feel like covering his accustomed miles, after that
brief but hectic encounter.   Coker stood looking after him,
till he was gone.

'Oh, gum!' murmured Coker.

That envelope was still in Quelch's pocket.   Mug,
certainly, would have had it this time, had not Coker
intervened.   Really, Coker couldn't have stood idly by,
while Quelch was hammered by a reckless ruffian.
But——!

He was through with Mug now.   Mug, certainly, would
never come within hitting distance of him again, if he could
help it.   That resource was at an end.   And it was Coker's
last resource.

'Oh, gum!' repeated Coker.

His last chance was gone.   Coker had completely
'dished' his own plans.   Completely, utterly, and
thoroughly, he had cooked his own goose!   Which, really,
was just like Coker!

CHAPTER 32

TEA WITH COKER

'I SAY, you fellows!'

'Hallo, hallo, hallo! Done your lines, Bunter?'

'Ha, ha, ha!'

The Famous Five chuckled. Billy Bunter frowned. They seemed to find the affair of Bunter's lines amusing. Bunter did not.

It was Saturday afternoon: a half-holiday at Greyfriars. Harry Wharton and Co. had been enjoying that half-holiday. Billy Bunter hadn't.

On a half-holiday, Billy Bunter did not yearn for the strenuous life. He did not want a pull in a boat, nor to join the fellows at the cricket nets, nor to spin on a bike, or ramble in the woods and lanes. But he did not want to sit in his study grinding out Latin lines.

And that was what the fat Owl had had to do, that summer's afternoon. Quelch had ordained that his three hundred lines were to be handed in that day. Billy Bunter did not want any more 'whops'; and the drastic measures adopted by the Famous Five had put paid to Coker as a resource in the matter of lines. So Bunter had had to write his lines himself.

Glumly and indignantly he had done so, and taken them in to Quelch. Now it was nearly tea-time: and Bunter, who was always ready for a meal before a meal was ready, for Bunter was in a state resembling that of a lion seeking what he might devour. He rolled out of the House to look for Coker, and came on the Famous Five, fresh and cheery from the river.

'Blessed if I see anything to cackle at,' grunted Bunter. 'I've been hours and hours and hours doing those beastly lines——'

'That's because you're a lazy, lazy, lazy Owl!' said Bob Cherry.

'Ha, ha, ha!'

'Beast! But I say, you fellows, seen Coker about?'

'Lots of times!' answered Bob.

'Oh, don't be a funny ass!' yapped Bunter. Three hundred lines had left the fat Owl a little irritable. Besides, he wanted his tea, and it was necessary to find Coker. 'Know where he is? I want him.'

'Does he want you?' grunted Johnny Bull.

'The wantfulness is probably not terrific' remarked Hurree Jamset Ram Singh.

'Give Coker a rest, you fat villain!' said Harry Wharton, frowning. 'If you're thinking of sticking him again for a study spread——'

'Oh, really, Wharton! I suppose Coker can ask a fellow to tea in his study if he likes! Anybody would think I was sponging on the chap, from the way you fellows talk!' exclaimed Bunter, indignantly.

'Oh, my hat!'

'Boot him!' growled Johnny Bull.

'Beast!'

Billy Bunter rolled away hastily. Harry Wharton and Co. exchanged eloquent looks. Bunter, evidently, was bent on 'sticking' Coker for another study spread. All the Co. agreed that it was time—high time—that Billy Bunter's career as a bad lad was brought to a stop. Coker, no doubt, had asked for it: but there was a limit, of which the fat Owl seemed quite unconscious. But so long as that envelope was in Quelch's pocket, Coker was under a fat grubby thumb: and there really seemed no help for the hapless Horace.

Having blinked round the quad, in vain, for Coker of the Fifth, Billy Bunter rolled into the House, and up to the Fifth-form studies. Coker's door was shut: but a powerful voice from within revealed that Horace was at home.

'It's getting too jolly thick, you fellows! That little beast Bunter came into the tuck-shop while I was there in break, and I had to stand him tarts. I tell you, it's getting too jolly thick.'

'Boot the fat tick, and chance it,' came Potter's voice.

'Yes, I would!' said Greene.

The grinning Owl in the passage heard a snort from Coker.

'Would you, Billy Greene! You jolly well wouldn't, if it was going to be the long jump if you did. And it jolly well would be, if Prout saw that limerick. Don't talk rot.'

Coker's temper, evidently, was not at its best. In fact, it was all very well for Potter and Greene to counsel him to boot the fat tick and chance it: but Coker was not in a position to take such chances.

Bunter, grinning, tapped on the door, and opened it. The three Fifth-form men, sitting round the study table, glanced at him. The look that Coker gave him was expressive. Indeed, Rhadamanthus, Aeacus, and the fabled Gorgon, combined, could hardly have bestowed such a look.

That expressive look did not worry Bunter. Really, he did not expect a welcoming smile from Coker! He rolled into the study.

Coker and Co. had sat down to tea. The supplies on the table, as usual in Coker's study, were ample. Billy Bunter gave the well-spread board an appreciative blink.

'Oh, here you are, Coker, old chap,' said **Bunter**, affably. 'I've been looking for you.'

Coker did not reply. He breathed hard, and he breathed deep: but speech seemed to fail him.

'I thought you'd like me to drop in to tea, old fellow,' went on Bunter, breezily. 'What about it?'

Coker made an inarticulate sound. Billy Bunter blinked round the study, for a chair. There were only three: all occupied. He blinked at Coker.

'Cut along and borrow a chair, will you?' he said. 'Dash it all, you might ask a fellow to sit down, Coker. Don't sit there like a stuffed dummy, old chap.'

Another inarticulate sound from Coker.

Potter and Greene rose from the table. If Coker was under the necessity of tolerating a cheeky fat fag in the study, they were not. Without a word, they walked out of the study, Potter banging the door.

'Good riddance to bad rubbish!' remarked Bunter, cheerfully. 'All the more for us, what? He, he, he.'

'Look here, Bunter——!' muttered Coker. How he restrained his almost frantic desire to smack Bunter's fat head right and left, he hardly knew. But he did!

'Well?' said Bunter, blinking at him. 'I've dropped in to tea. If you don't want me, you've only got to say so, of course. I'm not the fellow to butt in where I'm not wanted, I hope! Yes or no?'

Gladly Coker would have replied in the negative, punctuating his remarks with smacks on a fat head, or a boot on plump trousers. But he could not venture to do so. It was a subdued Coker, these days!

'Yes!' he gasped.

'Thanks, old chap!' Bunter sat down at the table. 'I'm going to stand a spread in my study, when my postal-order comes, and I won't forget to ask you, Coker. I say, that ham looks all right! Shove it this way, will you? I can manage the lot, if you don't want any.'

It was a well-spread board. But it thinned out, under Billy Bunter's operations. In matters of tuck, Bunter was a quick worker. Coker watched him, with deep, deep feelings. He did not seem to want to eat anything himself. He only looked as if he would rather have liked to eat Bunter!

Heedless of Coker's looks, the fat Owl demolished the foodstuffs. Bunter, if not Coker, was enjoying that spread. It was a fat, sticky, and happy Owl. But——

But there was going to be an interruption!

CHAPTER 33

LOST—AND FOUND

'BLESS my soul!'

'Hallo, hallo, hallo!' murmured Bob Cherry. 'What's up with Quelch?'

The Famous Five glanced round.

They were sauntering by the old elms, when that sudden and startled exclamation fell on their ears. They had not noticed that their respected 'beak', Mr. Quelch, was seated on one of the old benches under the shady branches. But they noticed him now.

Quelch looked perturbed.

He was groping in an inside pocket: and apparently he failed to find something he had expected to find there. He groped and groped: and then drew out the lining of the pocket. There was a gash in it: but nothing else.

'Bless my soul!' repeated Mr. Quelch. 'My book! Bless my soul!'

He glanced round quickly. There was nothing in the shape of a book to be seen on the ground anywhere round that bench.

'Wharton!'

'Yes, sir!' said Harry. 'Have you lost something, sir?'

'I have indeed, Wharton! My pocket edition of Horace —you have probably seen it in my hand sometimes——'

'Oh, yes, sir!'

'It seems to have slipped out of my pocket,' said Mr. Quelch. 'I find that a hole has worn in the lining. The book must have slipped through while I was walking in the

202

quadrangle.   Perhaps you boys would be kind enough to look for it.'

'Certainly, sir!' said the Famous Five, all together.

As a matter of fact, the Co. had just been thinking of going in to tea.   Tea in No. 1 Study was more attractive than hunting for a pocket edition of Quintus Horatius Flaccus, up and down and round about the Greyfriars quadrangle.   But they were obliging youths.   Moreover, a request from their form-master was rather in the nature of a Royal request;   tantamount to a command.   Quelch certainly expected them to be kind enough to look for that lost Flaccus.

'We'll look for it at once, sir,' said Bob Cherry.

'It must be somewhere about,' said Frank Nugent. 'We'll find it, sir.'

'We will look everywhere fully, esteemed sir!' said Hurree Jamset Ram Singh.

'It must be somewhere in the quadrangle,' said Mr. Quelch.   'It certainly was in my pocket when I left my study half-an-hour ago.   I shall be very much obliged if you find it.'

'Not at all, sir.'

'We'll find it.'

'Thank you,' said Mr. Quelch.   'Please lose no time. One moment!' he added, as the juniors were turning away. He seemed to have remembered something.

They turned back.

'I remember now, there was something else in that pocket,' said Mr. Quelch.   'It must have slipped through the lining with the book.   It was an envelope——'

'Oh!' ejaculated Bob.

'A plain envelope, with no superscription, containing a paper of some sort,' said Mr. Quelch.

o

'Oh! The one that tramp snatched on the beach the other day, sir?' exclaimed Bob.

'Yes, that is it,' said Mr. Quelch. 'Bunter asked me to mind it for him, and it must not be lost. Please look for it as well as for the book.'

'Oh, certainly, sir,' gasped Bob.

The Famous Five lost no time, as their form-master had requested. They hurried away to look for that book and that envelope. Mr. Quelch was left regarding that gash in the lining of his pocket, with a perturbed eye. After his walk in the quad, Quelch had sat down on that bench in the shade, and naturally reached for his pocket Horace, to give that great classic author the once-over once more. It was very disturbing to find that Quintus Horatius Flaccus was gone. Really, a book carried in a pocket was bound, sooner or later, to wear the lining, so what had happened was not really surprising. But it was perturbing.

However, there was still balm in Gilead, so to speak. Q. H. Flaccus might have dropped from his pocket while he was taking one of his walks abroad, in which case it would have been irretrievably lost. But as it had dropped within the precincts of Greyfriars, it only required looking for— and five obliging members of his form were looking for it.

Quelch, naturally, was more interested in Q. H. Flaccus than in Bunter's envelope. That little slim volume had been his companion for many years, and had many of his notes in the margins. It would have surprised him to know that those five members of his form were more interested in Bunter's envelope, than in Q. H. Flaccus! But undoubtedly they were!

'By gum!' breathed Bob, as soon as they were out of their form-master's hearing. 'That envelope—you know what's in it——'

'Coker's limerick!' said Harry.

'The absurb limerick of the esteemed and ridiculous Coker!' said Hurree Jamset Ram Singh, with a nod of his dusky head.

'If we find it, it's Coker's!' said Nugent.

'Coker's—no mistake about that,' agreed Johnny Bull.

'We've jolly well got to find it,' said Bob, emphatically. 'And when we've found it, it's going back where it belongs, what?'

'Yes, rather.'

'The ratherfulness is terrific.'

'Quelch doesn't know what's in that envelope,' went on Bob. 'But we jolly well know! That fat villain is making use of Quelch to keep that silly limerick safe, and hold it over Coker's silly head. This is where we put paid to him!'

'Hear, hear!'

'Coker's going to have his limerick back, as it belongs to him. Bunter can have the envelope, as it's his.'

'Ha, ha, ha!'

All the Co. were in accord on that point. That limerick was Coker's property, and Coker certainly was entitled to his own property. Only the envelope was Bunter's: and the fat Owl was welcome to it—after the limerick had been extracted from it!

'Come on,' said Bob. 'The sooner we spot it the better. Must be around somewhere where Quelch has been ambling.'

Round about and up and down they went, in eager search. They were keen enough to find the lost Flaccus, to oblige their form-master: but undoubtedly they were keener to discover that lost envelope.

'Hallo, hallo, hallo!' exclaimed Bob Cherry, a few minutes later.

They were hunting along the path between the old elms
and the school wall: a favourite walk of Quelch's. Bob's
eyes suddenly fell on a small object lying in the path. It
was a slim pocket volume.

He pounced on it, picked it up and handed it to Harry
Wharton.

'That's Quelch's, isn't it?' he asked.

'That's it,' said Harry, with a nod, as he looked at it.
'Pocket edition of Horace—here's Quelch's name in it, and
his scribble in the margins, too. We've found the jolly old
Horace but——'

'Well, the other thing can't be far away. Come on.'

'There's Prout,' said Johnny Bull, as a portly figure
appeared on the path ahead.

'Oh, my hat!' gasped Bob. 'Look!'

Mr. Prout was coming along the path, with his slow and
ponderous tread. He stopped suddenly, in his stately
walk. He stood staring at the ground, at some small object
at his feet.

The next moment, the juniors saw what that object was.
It was an envelope! Mr. Prout stared down at it, no doubt
surprised to see it there.

'Oh, gum!' breathed Bob. 'If Prout gets hold of it—
there's nothing written on it—suppose he opens it to see
whom it belongs to—oh, crikey!'

It was a critical moment!

If Prout saw the contents of that envelope—a description
of himself, in Coker's 'fist', as a pompous old duffer who
talked rot—undoubtedly all the fat would be in the fire!

And Prout was stooping, to pick up that envelope!

Bob Cherry did not stop to think. Coker had done him
a good turn, and he was going to do Coker one! He shot
forward like an arrow from a bow.

Stooping, to a gentleman of Mr. Prout's plump proportions, was a slow process. Slowly, he stooped, and reached a plump hand down to pick up that envelope. But the plump fingers had not touched it, when Bob Cherry crashed into him.

'Ohhh!' gasped Mr. Prout.

He rolled under that unexpected charge. He rolled right over. That envelope disappeared into Bob's pocket as he rolled.

'Ooooooh!' spluttered Mr. Prout. 'Ooooooh! What —what—who—who—upon my word! Ooogh!'

He sat up gurgling.

'Oh! Sorry, sir!' gasped Bob. 'Did—did—did I run into you, sir? Please let me help you up, sir! So sorry, sir.'

Truly, Bob was sorry that he had had to up-end Mr. Prout, to get possession of that envelope.

'Ooogh! You—you—you utterly stupid boy!' gurgled Mr. Prout. 'How dare you race along the path in that reckless manner, Cherry? How dare you be so reckless, Cherry—so utterly unthinking and reckless! I shall report this to your form-master, Cherry! Ooogh! Upon my word! Woooh!'

'Sorry, sir——'

'Ooogh! You are the most thoughtless and clumsy boy in the school, Cherry! Only the other day you rushed into my deck-chair, just as you have now rushed into me. Are you blind?'

'Oh! No, sir! I—I——'

'You must learn, Cherry, not to rush about the place in so reckless and disorderly a manner! Oooh! You have actually caused me to fall! Ooogh! I shall certainly report your foolish thoughtlessness to Mr. Quelch! Wooogh.'

The Co. came running up.

They gathered round Mr. Prout, dutifully and sympathetically helping that ponderous gentleman to his feet. Bob Cherry discreetly backed off the scene, and disappeared: while Harry Wharton, Frank Nugent, Johnny Bull, and Hurree Jamset Ram Singh gave Mr. Prout first-aid. The Fifth-form master stood gasping, and gasping and gasping, as if he would never leave off gasping.

'Ooogh! Stupid—clumsy—unthinking—ooogh! I am quite breathless—oooh! That stupid—clumsy boy—oooh! Wharton!'

'Yes, sir!'

'I was about to pick up an envelope, when that clumsy unthinking boy crashed into me. A letter, I think—someone must have dropped it. Please look for it! I do not seem to see it now.'

'We'll look for it, sir.'

'Certainly, sir.'

The Co. were careful not to smile. They knew where that envelope was, if Mr. Prout did not. However, they proceeded industriously to look for it! Oddly enough, as it seemed to Mr. Prout, it was not to be found. Which really was not very surprising, as it was in Bob Cherry's pocket, and Bob was on his way to Coker's study in the Fifth.

CHAPTER 34

BOB'S YOUR UNCLE

TAP!

Billy Bunter did not heed that tap at the door of Coker's study.

Bunter was busy. He was dealing with a dish of cream cakes. Bunter liked cream cakes. They were going down the fattest neck at Greyfriars almost like oysters. Heedless of taps at the door, Billy Bunter went on with the cream cakes.

But Coker glanced round at the door, with a frowning brow. Coker did not want visitors, to behold a fat fag feasting in his study. He would just have hated any Fifth-form man to look in, at the moment.

The door opened.

A cheery, ruddy face, surmounted by a mop of flaxen hair, appeared in the doorway. Coker glared at it.

It was rather a relief that it was not a Fifth-form man. But Coker was in no mood to be patient with a Remove junior butting in. One Remove junior in his study was more than enough for Coker. He had to stand Bunter. But with Bob Cherry he was more disposed to adopt his short way with fags.

Billy Bunter gave Bob a careless blink. Why Bob had looked in, the fat Owl neither knew nor cared. He was not interested in Bob. His interest was concentrated on cream cakes.

'Hallo, hallo, hallo!' began Bob, cheerily. 'I——'

'Get out!' roared Coker.

'But I've come here——'

'I said get out.'

'Do let a chap speak!' urged Bob.   'I've got something here——'

'I don't care what you've got!   Get out before I kick you down the passage!' roared Coker.

'You silly ass!' roared back Bob.   'I've got something of yours that I've picked up in the quad——'

'Rot! I've not dropped anything in the quad! I did drop something a week ago, and that fat villain Bunter picked it up——'

'He, he, he!' came through a barrage of cream cake.

'I know all about that, Coker.   The fat tick put it in an envelope and asked Quelch to mind it for him——'

'You needn't come here and tell me what I know already. Shut that door after you.'

Coker made a stride towards the junior in the doorway. Evidently, his short way with fags was about to be put into operation!

Bob snatched the envelope from his pocket and held it up!

'Look at that!' he bawled.

Coker stared at it.

'What's that?' he snapped.   'If you've picked up a letter, it's not mine—nothing to do with me, you young ass.'

'It's not a letter——'

'I don't care what it is!   I'll jolly well boot you down the passage for your cheek in shoving in here.   Now——'

'It's your limerick!' shrieked Bob: just in time.

Coker jumped.

'WHAT?' he stuttered.

'Quelch had a hole in the lining of his pocket, and it dropped out——'

'Oh, crumbs!' gasped Coker.

'Oh, crikey!' came like an echo from Billy Bunter. Quite suddenly, Bunter ceased operations on the cream cakes! Those cream cakes were good—quite good—but they seemed to have lost their savour, all of a sudden. The fat Owl blinked at Bob Cherry in consternation.

'Mum-mum-my limerick!' stuttered Coker.

He seemed hardly able to believe it! Indeed, he hardly could! He fairly goggled at that envelope in Bob's hand. It really seemed to Coker altogether too much good fortune for his limerick to come home to roost, as it were, in his own study!

'You see, Quelch had a book—a pocket Horace—in the same pocket,' explained Bob. 'It must have worn the lining —anyhow, both of them fell out while he was trotting round, and he asked us to look for them. He will get his jolly old Horace back, but this belongs to you—I mean, what's inside it belongs to you—the envelope's Bunters——'

'Oh, crikey!' gasped Bunter.

'Better look in it to make sure!' added Bob.

Coker took the envelope, with a hand that almost trembled. All his own efforts to recover that lost limerick had failed. He had as good as given up hope. And now——!

He jerked the envelope open. From within he drew a crumpled sheet of paper. He unfolded it. He stared at it. Even yet he could hardly believe in his good luck. But there it was. There, under his eyes, in his own rugged scrawling fist, was the limerick——

> There's a pompous old duffer named Prout,
> Enormously podgy and stout,
>   He talks awful rot,
>   And he never knows what
> He is talking and talking about!

There it was—quite sufficient to get Horace Coker, of the Fifth, 'sacked' if it met the eyes of Mr. Prout and the Head! But it was not going to meet those eyes now! It was safe back in Horace Coker's hands: and even Coker was not thinking now of typing it on Quelch's typewriter for his form-master's behoof. Coker had had enough—more than enough—of that limerick! He hadn't the slightest desire to carry on as a limericker! All he wanted was to see the last of that limerick!

'Oh!' he gasped. 'It—it—it—it's it!'

'It's it all right!' agreed Bob Cherry. 'Hadn't you better put a match to it, Coker?'

'I don't need a fag to tell me what to do,' retorted Coker. However, he scratched a match, and put it to the limerick. That disrespectful description of Prout burned away in his fingers. He pitched the last charred fragment into the grate.

'All serene now—and Bob's your uncle,' chuckled Bob Cherry. 'Better steer clear of limericks after this, Coker.'

'When I want advice from a fag, I'll ask for it!' snapped Coker. Then he made an effort. 'I'm jolly glad of this, Cherry! Thanks.'

'Not at all,' answered Bob. 'Always glad to help a silly fathead who hasn't as much sense as a bunny rabbit.'

Bob shut the door and departed, with that: which was just as well.

Coker fixed his eyes on Billy Bunter.

Bunter had risen from the table. There were still cream cakes on the dish: and Bunter had intended to finish them, to the last spot of cream. But he was not thinking of finishing them now. He was eyeing Coker, through his big spectacles, with well-founded uneasiness. Billy Bunter was not, perhaps, very bright: but he was bright enough to realize that his hold on Coker was gone with that limerick. For nearly a week, Coker's study had been to that bad lad like unto a land flowing with milk and honey. But the glory, so to speak, had now departed from the House of Israel. It had been a most attractive study: so long as that envelope was safe in Mr. Quelch's pocket and that limerick hanging over Horace Coker's head like the sword of Damocles. Now all its attractions had vanished—and the unscrupulous fat Owl was only anxious to escape from it without a boot behind him as he went.

Watching Coker like an alarmed and wary Owl, Bunter sidled towards the door. Coker stepped between him and the door, and he had to stop.

'Don't go, Bunter!' said Coker, grimly.

'I—I—I've got to see a chap!' stammered Bunter. 'I—I——'

'That chap will have to wait a bit!' grinned Coker. He could grin, now.

'I—I mean, I—I've got to see Quelch!' gasped Bunter. 'I—I can't keep my beak waiting, Coker! I—I say, lemme pass, will you?'

'Not just yet!' grinned Coker. 'You haven't finished your tea, Bunter.'

'I—I'd rather not finish it now, Coker! I—I——'

'Not another cream cake?' asked Coker, genially.

'Nunno! I—I—I'd rather go——!' mumbled Bunter.

'Yes: I fancy you would!' said Coker, with a nod. 'Well, you're going all right—but I'm going to boot you round the study, first——'

'I—I—I say——!'

'And then I'm going to dribble you down the passage,' went on Coker. 'I rather think that you won't butt into my study again in a hurry, Bunter! What do you think?'

Billy Bunter blinked longingly at the door. The tables
had been turned, with a vengeance! He had had Coker at
his beck and call—feeding from his fat hand, as it were—
but now——! Now, having called the tune, it was time to
pay the piper! No doubt it was a case of 'Bob's your
uncle' with Horace Coker, now that that limerick was
reduced to ashes. But it was far from being 'Bob's your
uncle' with Billy Bunter. The hapless fat Owl was feeling
like Daniel in the lion's den. From the bottom of his fat
heart, he wished that he had taken the advice of Harry
Wharton and Co. and 'chucked' his career as a 'bad lad' at
an earlier stage. But it was too late now. After the feast
came the reckoning.

He had no chance of getting at the door. He backed
round the table, to place that article of furniture between
him and Coker.

But it booted not!

Coker, grinning, came round the table after him.

Thud!

'Yaroooh!'

A large foot landed on plump trousers. Billy Bunter
roared, and dodged frantically. But he dodged in vain.
Coker had told him that he was going to boot him round
the study. Coker was a man of his word. How many
times that large foot landed on plump trousers, Bunter
hardly knew—it seemed to him like scores, if not hundreds.
Frantic yells echoed among the Fifth-form studies. When,
at last, Coker threw open the door, a yelling fat Owl bolted
wildly into the passage. But even then he was not done
with Coker. The grinning Horace followed him out, and
dribbled him down the passage, as far as the landing.
There, at last, Billy Bunter escaped, bolting down the stairs.

'Come to my study again when you want some more,

Bunter!' bawled Coker.   And he walked back to his study
chuckling: a very cheery Coker!

Billy Bunter was not likely to revisit that study!   The
largest and most luscious parcel that had ever arrived from
Aunt Judy would hardly have tempted him near it.

CHAPTER 35

ENOUGH FOR BUNTER!

'HALLO, hallo, hallo!'

'Ow! wow!'

'Enjoying life, old fat man?'

'Yow-ow-ow!'

Really, the Famous Five could hardly have supposed that Billy Bunter was enjoying life, when they came on him in the quad. Wriggling and mumbling and squeaking did not indicate enjoyment.

It was a dismal and disconsolate Bunter.

He blinked dolorously at five grinning faces.

'Had a good time with Coker?' asked Bob.

'Ow! wow! wow!'

'Ha, ha, ha!'

'Blessed if I see anything to cackle at,' moaned Bunter. 'That beast Coker cut up rusty——'

'Did he?' grinned Bob. 'I wonder why?'

'Ha, ha, ha!'

'He kicked me——!'

'Serve you jolly well right, you fat tick,' said Harry Wharton. 'If Quelch hadn't lost that envelope, and if we hadn't found it, you'd still be sticking him for tuck——'

'Bad lad!' said Bob.

'The badfulness is terrific,' said Hurree Jamset Ram Singh, shaking his dusky head. 'Honesty is the cracked pitcher that goes longest to the well, as the English proverb remarks, my esteemed and idiotic Bunter.'

'Ow! wow! wow!'